OUTPOST 28

ISSUE 2

99/100

MARCH 2018

Cover art "Windowpane" by Dean Kuhta.

ISBN 10: 0-692-08167-4
ISBN 13: 978-0-692-08167-9

Published by Elvelon Press.

www.deankuhta.com

Printed in the United States of America.

Book design by Dean Kuhta.

10 9 8 7 6 5 4 3 2 1

OUTPOST 28

Issue 2   March 2018

Outpost 28 is published twice a year by Elvelon Press. Single copy: $9.00. Payment accepted via the official website at www.deankuhta.com/outpost28.php. Please email outpost28@deankuhta.com for all artwork or writing submissions.

Half of all proceeds go to helping the homeless in Richmond, VA.

PHANTOM ECHOES, VOL. II

Editorial by Dean Kuhta

Welcome to the second issue of Outpost 28! I am so thankful, once again, to have the opportunity to collaborate with so many talented writers, artists, and musicians on this amazing project. It's been a few years, but Outpost 28 has finally clawed its way back from a dark and deep slumber to be resurrected once again! Back with a disturbing vengeance, this second issue features soul-swallowing horror, phantasmic darkness, and a suitable dose of brain-munching zombies. The illustrations lurking within these cosmic pages are even more sinister and foul. The literary talent drips from each short story.

The mission of Outpost 28 is to serve as a focal point for positive energy. What the heck does that rubbish mean, you ask? It means that the function of this endeavor is to harness the collective creativity of the artists and authors, and channel that energy to the readers. As a result of this artistic exchange, the ultimate goal is to donate half of all proceeds to the homeless. The idea of collaborating with artists and authors from all over the world (Portugal, Pakistan, Canada, France, UK, and the US) to produce a magazine that is enjoyed by others, and to use that revenue to help those in need, is a worthwhile achievement.

Outpost 28 strives to carry on the atmosphere of the old pulp magazines from the '50s and '60s such as *Weird Tales* and *Amazing Stories*, as well as the tradition of collaborative writing and artwork. We hope you enjoy the short stories, illustrations, and interviews in this second issue!

-Dean, February 23, 2018

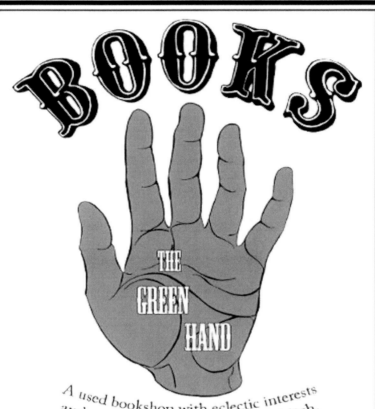

THREE CHEERS FOR SWEET REVENGE

by Christa Carmen

For Claire, for the Gothic beetle brooch...

artwork by David Bonneywell

From: Kimberly Fairhurst kim_fairhurst@gmail.com
Date: Mon, May 05, 2008 at 10:31 AM
Subject: Re: Are you there yet?
To: Kerri Kusa kerrik0917@gmail.com

Ker,

We made it! The flight was relatively painless; I nabbed a seat by myself, so I read and slept without having to suffer through small talk with anyone. I can't believe I'm here. No, I can't believe I'm here and you're not. I'm glad you like your new position, and I know you said that you're over the bullshit, but it still sucks you left two months before Centennial okayed a trip for the whole group to travel to the UK. We should have been on this trip together. Just so you know, none of the analysts will even look at Brent since he took the job. He may have won, but he didn't play fair, and what goes around comes around, clichéd as that may sound. I hope I didn't upset you by bringing it up. I just wanted to let you know that he's already reaping what he sowed within the group, and I can't imagine his reception will be any better with the UK colleagues tomorrow. Our three-day meeting starts then, after which I have Thursday and Friday off for sight-seeing. Saturday, we fly back to the States. Sunday, you and I are having brunch to catch up! The hotel is in Canterbury, a twenty-minute drive from Sandwich. From what I could see from the taxi, there are dozens of shops and cafes to check out. We're going out to lunch as soon as everyone gets settled, so I should unpack at least a few things, and freshen up. I'll write more later...miss you already!

Much love,
Kim

From: Kimberly Fairhurst kim_fairhurst@gmail.com
Date: Mon, May 05, 2008 at 9:23 PM
Subject: Re: Are you there yet?
To: Kerri Kusa kerrik0917@gmail.com

Ker,
Did you read my email from earlier today? You're five hours behind, so you should've gotten it by now. Whatever time it is there, it's bedtime here; I have to combat this jetlag and get some rest before tomorrow. You know how I said the meeting was Monday through Wednesday? Only colleagues on the extended leadership team have to attend the second half of the third day, so I'll have another afternoon to go exploring! I promise to push Brent into the Thames if an opportunity presents itself. I hope you don't mind I'm going to email you with the same frequency I would if it was any other work week. I expect the same from you, so write back, woman!

Xo
-Kim

P.S. Have the US papers been covering a story out of Kent over the past twenty-four hours, of a fourteen-year-old girl who hanged herself as a result of some suicide cult romanticized by an 'emo' rock band she admired? It's a circus here because of it, protestors demanding that the band make a statement, hundreds of kids dressed in black, holding posters to support the emo culture. It's been impossible to ignore; the story's on the cover of every newspaper, and every television in the hotel lobby has been tuned to the coverage. Anyhow, I was curious if you'd heard anything about it. Goodnight!

From: Kimberly Fairhurst kim_fairhurst@gmail.com
Date: Tue, May 06, 2008 at 6:01 PM
Subject: UK update
To: Kerri Kusa kerrik0917@gmail.com

Kerriiiiiiii,
Look who finally got around to writing back. I shouldn't tease, I'm grateful for the pictures of Monte Catso, and that you're pet-sitting for me in the first place. I hope you remembered his little overnight bag. You know from whence he takes his name; the Count will exact revenge on you if he feels his treatment has been unjust!

On a darker note, I saw Larry today. I don't know how I'd convinced myself that I wouldn't run into him while we were here. Ker, it's awful, having to watch the whole team fawn over him. When he smiles, all I can see is my sister's bruised and bloodied face. When he shakes someone's hand, I see his hands wrapped around my sister's throat. I know she said she would press charges, but it's been two months already, and she insists she 'needs more time.' Shannon also swears she doesn't blame me, but if I hadn't asked her to meet us for drinks that night, she would never have met that abusive piece of shit in the first place.

As much as I want to see him punished, part of me wishes he'd apply for the new position, and transfer to the UK permanently. At least there'd be less of a chance of him hurting her again. He could have killed her, and she's too traumatized to go to the police, so he's walking around like the master of the universe, sniffing out his next victim.

I should get ready for dinner, but I haven't filled you in on the latest with Meghan Martin; she's the girl I told you about yesterday. The news broadcasts continue to cover her death around the clock, and today they released the information that it was her mother who found the body. Meghan's friend had been visiting, and after she left, Mrs. Martin realized that the same song—some morbid thing about death and graveyards—had been playing on repeat for over an hour. She went upstairs to check on her daughter. Meghan had poisoned herself before stepping off her desk with a makeshift noose around her neck. I don't know how that poor woman will ever recover.

It's sad, how committed she was to ending her life, but also a little strange. If a fourteen-year-old girl was motivated to kill herself because her favorite band wears black and sings about death, she wouldn't exactly have the courage of her convictions, would she? It makes more sense if she'd taken a modest amount of sleeping pills and called 911. You know, a suicide attempt.

That way, she'd have the respect of the emo community (if that really is what they're all about), but she'd also have her life.

Blame it on the dullness of the meeting today, but Meghan's story has really grabbed me. The band at the center of the controversy released a statement, that while their music may be "rooted in the darker aspects of the human experience," it no more glamorized death than did the tragedies of Shakespeare. They also expressed their condolences to the girl's family, which I thought was good of them. Have you looked up the story online yet? I was going to send you some links, but I was supposed to be downstairs for dinner five minutes ago! Got to run!

-Kim

From: Kimberly Fairhurst kim_fairhurst@gmail.com
Date: Wed, May 07, 2008 at 9:46 AM
Subject: UK update
To: Kerri Kusa kerrik0917@gmail.com

I wish I'd thought to have Verizon change my plan while I was here, so I could call you without it costing a fortune. It appears I'm to get my wish, because not only did Larry apply for the senior analyst position, they announced last night that he got it. Lawrence Brockmeyer will be moving to the United Kingdom within the month. Believe it or not, that's not the most interesting thing I'm writing to you about.

Candace knew I was upset that Larry will likely skirt responsibility indefinitely for what he did to Shannon, so she offered to stay out with me to have a few drinks. We went to a bar across from the restaurant called Seven Stars. It was empty, except for a group huddled around a table in the corner. Candace's plan to get me drunk enough to forget my worries backfired, since Drew Dalton had tagged along, and was going on and on about how excited he was for Larry to be in the Sandwich office, and how he couldn't wait to buy the guy a drink. Candace was a saint, drawing the idiot into another topic of conversation, while I guzzled my drink and tried not to cry. The group in the corner had dispersed, but a somber-looking woman drifted over to the bar and slid onto a stool a few seats from my own.

I said hello and made some stupid comment about it being okay that I was drinking on a weeknight because I was on vacation. She asked me where I was from, and when I told her, said that it was okay that she was drinking on a weeknight because her sister was dead.

I almost fell off the barstool. My face burned, and I stammered out an apology. "It's fine," she said. "It's not like we haven't been reminded of it every waking hour with all the media coverage." Her words penetrated the fog of a brain already hampered by too much alcohol, but I said nothing, rationalizing that the probability of finding myself next to Meghan Martin's sister was too unlikely.

"Have you seen the coverage of the fourteen-year-old suicide victim?" she asked. Despite my voyeurism over the past two days, or maybe because of it, I played dumb. "I heard some hubbub on the street this morning," was as much as I admitted to. She sighed in a forlorn, exhausted way, and I wondered if I should excuse myself and leave her to her grief. As I tried to get the bartender's attention, the woman took a swig of beer, clanked the bottle down on the bar top, and said, "You're from America, so you wouldn't sell my secrets to the Daily Mail, would you?" I looked at her, taken aback, and she said, "I'm sorry. I don't know how I'm going to come to terms with this if I don't talk to someone about it."

She reached out to shake my hand, told me her name was Rachel Martin. I introduced myself, said that I wished I was meeting her under different circumstances. She let out a humorless bark of laughter. "Here you said you were on vacation. I'm sure you were dying to be cornered by someone whose idea of an icebreaker was to tell you their sister was dead."

I gestured to Candace and Drew, who'd moved to a high-top at the center of the room, engaged in what looked like a heated debate. "I won't be missed," I told her. "I got some bad news myself this evening. Nothing to rival your tragedy, but if you're looking for someone to whom you can relay your troubles, I'd be happy to listen." She sipped from her beer again and looked as if she might cry. Then, she shook herself, signaled the bartender for another drink, and began to tell her story.

"Meghan was angst-ridden, but no more than your average teenager. Her obsession with the macabre always seemed innocent, a personality quirk more than a propensity for self-harm or Satanism." The bartender took her empty beer bottle and set a fresh one down in front of her. "We went through her room yesterday, found all the things we dreaded finding. The things the papers are saying that parents of kids interested in these 'suicide cults' should watch out for. A Ouija Board. Tarot cards. Black candles, and a book about witchcraft. Black everything. Black clothes, black jewelry, black combat boots. Makeup she must have hidden from my mother, bone-white face powder and black lipstick. She must have put that stuff on after getting to school, because while my mother had seen her in heavy eyeliner, she wouldn't have let her out of the house looking like Morticia Addams."

I smiled, and she went on. "We found dozens of CDs. My Chemical Romance was her favorite. We also found her journal." She paused. Before I realized what was happening, she was crying hard enough for tears to have soaked the collar of her blouse. "That's what I don't understand," she exclaimed. "From her journal, Meg didn't seem depressed at all! Sure, she wrote some dark shit. What she imagined her funeral would be like, and if the boy she had a crush on would miss her if she was gone. A séance she performed with her friends—I skipped most of that. Which of her black dresses she thought she looked the best in. It was all so...playful! Experimental. It was darkness suffused with hope!"

Rachel picked up her beer and set it down again without drinking. We were both quiet for a long time. Finally, bereft, she said, "I could have it all wrong. Maybe the fascination had become an obsession. Maybe all those images of death had warped her mind."

Her sadness was like a living thing. I wanted to comfort her, which is what I was probably going for when I said, "I used to work at a substance abuse facility. At first, it was rewarding, and I threw myself into the work. But sometimes a patient who was doing well, whose drug screens were clean, well, sometimes I'd get pulled into my supervisor's office and given the news that they'd overdosed and died."

I don't know why I told her this, Ker. I couldn't stand her grief, couldn't stand picturing Meghan's room full of dried flowers and black candles, the dichotomy of the hopeful journal ramblings and her death, and I just blurted it out.

"You worked at a drug dependency clinic?" Rachel asked, curious. I told her I had, that it was years ago now, practically in another life. "I guess those trips to my supervisor's office affected me more than I realized, because I switched careers completely. I work for a tech company now." Rachel didn't seem to be listening. "Did you go to school to become a counselor?" she asked. I told her that I had. "You can work at some places in the States with a certificate," I said. "But I got a degree."

She was looking at me like I was going to sell her secrets to the Daily Mail after all, but as it turned out, I misjudged that look. "Do you think you could look at Meghan's journal?" she asked, her voice suddenly filled with a terrible sort of optimism. I asked her what for. "To see if you think she was depressed. To read through some of that awful Séance stuff."

"I can't...I'm not...I shouldn't...," I stuttered. Her response to that was, "I don't think you realize how much the press has turned Meghan's death into a circus. It's the angry, God-fearing folks against the Satan-worshipping emo freaks. Any mental health professional we contacted, I wouldn't trust them not to go right to the press. You..." she pointed her beer bottle in my direction. I heard Drew laugh, and turned to see Candace fiddling with the jukebox. "You're not even from here! You happened to be in this bar. You have a mental health license...!"

"It's expired," I broke in, determined to be clear just how unqualified I was for this task. "It doesn't matter," Rachel insisted. "It's not for some source for the newspaper. It's for me and my family, for our own peace of mind." "I'm here on a work trip," I said quietly. "I have to go back to the hotel with them." I gestured at my colleagues. "Then tomorrow," she said, her tone suggesting that when was the only issue left to discuss. Candace and Drew had gotten up and were shrugging into their coats. Candace caught my eye and raised an eyebrow. I nodded, stood, retrieved my coat as well. "I..." At the look on Rachel's face, her skin so pale she could have been in one of the emo music videos her sister had so adored, I stopped. "Here's my card," I whispered, placing it on the bar with the money for my drinks. "My cell is on there. Call me tomorrow and I'll see what I can do."

I told Candace and Drew that Rachel and I had been discussing interesting places to visit while in London. It's almost two in the morning now, and I'm exhausted, but stone cold sober. I can't believe I ended up in the same bar as Meghan Martin's sister. I can't believe she wants my help. My head is spinning, but I'm glad I got this all down. I have no idea what time she's going to call tomorrow. I hope this doesn't end up being a mistake...

From: Kimberly Fairhurst kim_fairhurst@gmail.com
Date: Thu, May 08, 2008 at 12:30 PM
Subject: Re: UK update
To: Kerri Kusa kerrik0917@gmail.com

Kerri,

Sheesh, from your email, you'd have thought I was going to summon a demon, not read a few passages of a teenager's journal! I just woke up—good thing my agenda includes little more than sight-seeing today—but Rachel hasn't even called, so stop worrying! Scratch Catso behind the ears for me and, oh, there's my cell now...got to run!

From: Kimberly Fairhurst kim_fairhurst@gmail.com
Date: Fri, May 09, 2008 at 3:15 AM
Subject: Meghan Martin
To: Kerri Kusa kerrik0917@gmail.com

I'm at the Martin's place. We're about to go upstairs so Rachel can show me Meghan's journal. I'll let you know when I'm back at the hotel. Wish me luck...

-K

From: Kimberly Fairhurst kim_fairhurst@gmail.com
Date: Fri, May 09, 2008 at 3:15 AM
Subject: Re: Meghan Martin
To: Kerri Kusa kerrik0917@gmail.com

Kerri,

I'm sorry I didn't answer when you called. At the time, it would have been impossible to talk, and now, I'm not sure I can put into words what happened, or what we saw.

When I wrote earlier that my cell was going off, it was Rachel, calling to let me know she'd be at my hotel when the last of the reporters and news crews outside her parents' home had gone. At 8:25, I climbed into her black Volkswagen Beetle, and by the time we walked up the steep stone steps and through an unlit foyer, her parents had retired for the night. Rachel said she hadn't told them about me after all, that she didn't want to get their hopes up. They were on a bunch of medication to help them sleep after the shock of losing their daughter.

Rachel was right about Meghan's obsession with black. A black rug covered the hardwood floor, and black tapestries had been hung on the walls. The bedspread was black, as were the curtains. The only splashes of color were three red glass roses in a black vase, red velvet ribbons tied around the bases of the lamps, and red candles ensnared by wreaths of black bouquets.

Rachel stood at the center of this sea of black until I asked if I could see the journal, which she retrieved from Meghan's desk, along with a framed photo. "This was Meghan," she said, pointing out a slight, smiling teen. "Those were her best friends, Joan and Piper." She handed me the black velvet notebook, held closed by a thin piece of wire ending in a delicate, paper rose. I caught Rachel's eye. She nodded, so I unwound the wire and opened to the first page.

Rachel was right about the journal too. The first few entries were indicative of any fourteen-year-old girl. That is, until I got to the part about the séance. Rather than explain it, I'll let you experience it as I did, through Meghan's words. At one point while I was reading, Rachel had to excuse herself to find a box of tissues. While she was gone, I took photos of the pertinent pages on my phone. Perhaps you will come away with a less disturbing opinion of these events than I.

I doubt it.

April 6th, 2008

I have to fix my makeup. I tried not to cry when that awful Bridget ripped the crucifix from my neck. It hurt, don't get me wrong, but it was more the fact that half of last period math class saw it happen, and heard her call me, 'goth girl geek.' Hayden caught me by my locker. He fixed the clasp of my necklace with his pocketknife, which was sweet of him. He left when he saw Joan and Piper coming, said that Joan always looks at him funny, but his presence in that moment made me feel less alone.

Still, Helena will make everything all right. If we succeed in raising her spirit, Helena will avenge us against bullies like Bridget. Helena, whose rage at her lover's betrayal was such that her soul turned black. Helena, trapped in a revenge-fueled purgatory. Helena, the patron saint of the lost, the persecuted. We first found out about Helena from Joan's sister, Heather. Heather was friends with Helena's great niece, who'd been bequeathed her great aunt's brooch years after Helena's death in a car crash orchestrated by her lover. Legend had it that whoever attempted to summon Helena's spirit while possessing the brooch would be granted the revenge they sought.

When Joan and Piper arrived, the first thing I did was make sure Joan had succeeded in sneaking the brooch from her sister's jewelry box. (It hadn't surprised me in the slightest to learn that Joan's sister had stolen the brooch from her so-called friend. Joan could be mean, but her sister was downright ruthless. That was the moment the plan to raise Helena had taken shape.)

Joan grinned, and held the brooch out to me. It was beautiful but...strange. Its curves and reflective surfaces caused it to appear very much alive, like a gothic beetle from the underworld. We sat in a circle, and I placed my fingers on the planchette. In a voice I hoped did not waver, I said:

"Helena of the wronged, we three ask of thee, a sign that you are here. We ask that you provide for us only that which was denied you: a chance to navigate the world free from victimization and despair, and perhaps, should you seek it, the punishment of those who have done us wrong."

Journal, I swear on everything, that planchette moved on its own. It moved like something had come up from the depths of Hell to chase it.

Y-O-U-T-H-R-E-E-I-W-I-L-L-S-E-R-V-E-T-H-E-E-I-F-O-N-L-Y-Y-O-U-W-I-L-L-F-R-E-E-M-E

"How do we free you?" I asked. Joan and Piper were shaking like trees in a hurricane, but I glared at them to keep them focused.

A-D-R-O-P-O-F-B-L-O-O-D-F-R-O-M-E-A-C-H-O-N-T-H-E-M-I-R-R-O-R-S-U-R-F-A-C-E
P-L-A-C-E-T-H-E-M-I-R-R-O-R-B-E-N-E-A-T-H-T-H-E-B-O-A-R-D-S-A-Y-M-Y-N-A-M-E-T-H-R-E-E-T-I-M-E-S

We used the brooch to prick our fingers, squeezed the blood onto the surface of my hand mirror, and placed the board atop it. We gripped one another's hands.

We said her name three times. The planchette began to move so fast we could hardly keep up with what it said:

I-M-H-E-R-E-A-N-E-W-B-U-T-N-O-T-F-O-R-Y-O-U

T-H-E-R-E-V-E-N-G-E-Y-O-U-S-E-E-K-I-S-N-O-T-F-O-R-T-H-E-M-E-E-K

R-A-T-H-E-R-T-H-E-O-N-E-W-H-O-S-E-N-E-E-D-I-S-M-O-R-E

T-H-A-N-A-L-L-T-H-E-O-T-H-E-R-S-A-T-T-H-E-B-O-A-R-D

There was a sound at the window, but when we turned, there was nothing there but an overgrown tree branch scraping against the glass. Joan began to wail then, like something was burrowing into her brain. I tried to clap my hand over her mouth to keep her from waking my parents, but air, or smoke, or some sort of...presence, whizzed past my fingers, seemingly sucked into her throat, and I pulled back.

It ended as quickly as it had begun. The planchette grew still. I tried to ask Joan and Piper what they thought it meant, that thing about revenge being for the one at the board who wanted it more, but something wasn't right. Joan's eyes were glassy, and when she looked at me, they narrowed and grew darker. Her expression scared me, so I smacked her in the arm and told her to quit it. She said she was tired and didn't want to sleep over anymore. She called her mother to come get her and was gone twenty minutes later.

"Do you think she knows Hayden asked you out?" Piper said before we went to sleep. "How could she?" I snapped. But, I wonder. Like I said, Joan can be mean. I'd hate to think of what she'd do if she discovered that not only had Hayden asked me out, but that I'd said yes. We're going to a My Chemical Romance concert at the end of May.

I'm so happy I could die!

I was so absorbed by Meghan's journal, I hadn't realized Rachel had been reading over my shoulder. "Come on," she said, and I jumped, startled at her proximity, at her breath upon my neck. She held a hand mirror up, and I stared at my pale complexion in its oval face. There was a smear at the center of it.

"Here," Rachel said, and handed me a metallic brooch. I started to stutter out a protest, but Rachel gave me a hard look, and the words died in my throat. "My sister wasn't crazy," Rachel said. "If she said those things happened, I believe her. And I need to see it for myself." Feeling chastised, and more than a little ill, I followed her to the center of the raven-black rug.

At Rachel's urging, I pricked my finger with the pin. Blood fell onto the mirror, drops remaining intact like languid ladybugs upon the glass. I handed the brooch to Rachel, sucking at my finger as she repeated the ritual.
Rachel positioned the Ouija board over the mirror. She held out her hands. I took them, but panic welled in my throat, and I said, "Rachel, maybe we shouldn't—"

"Helena. Helena. Helena," was her reply.

A sudden bang as the wind blew a tree branch against the window. It scratched across the glass, the sound as sinister as footsteps in a purportedly empty place. The air in the room grew bitter cold. Meghan's CD player switched on and began playing from the bookshelf. Rachel pulled my hands down until my fingers came to rest on the planchette next to hers. The glass-eyed piece began to move, whip-fast, but I was hawk-eyed in my terror:

I-M-H-E-R-E-A-N-E-W-B-U-T-N-O-T-F-O-R-Y-O-U

T-H-E-R-E-V-E-N-G-E-Y-O-U-S-E-E-K-I-S-N-O-T-F-O-R-T-H-E-M-E-E-K

R-A-T-H-E-R-T-H-E-O-N-E-W-H-O-S-E-N-E-E-D-I-S-M-O-R-E

T-H-A-N-A-N-Y-O-T-H-E-R-A-T-T-H-E-B-O-A-R-D

Rachel's face was bloodless, but she had the wherewithal to say, "What happened to my sister? She asked you for revenge against those that had harmed her and you did nothing. She took her own life! How can you call yourself the patron saint of anything?" I-A-M-S-A-I-N-T-O-F-N-O-T-H-I-N-G-P-A-T-R-O-N-O-F-N-O-O-N-E-B-U-T-M-Y-S-E-L-F

As the planchette flew, I saw movement from the other side of the room. When I looked up, there was...God, Kerri, there was something at the window. Something I think I will go mad for having seen.

It was a woman. Perhaps she was Helena, perhaps she was something older, darker, far more terrible than any troubled teen or goth band could conceive of. The creature oscillated among many forms: a haggard witch, whose lies fell from her lips like insects shedding carapaces; once, I saw my own reflection, with fire-red eyes and sunken cheeks. For the briefest of moments, the thing at the window was beautiful. She was Meghan's Helena, goddess of revenge. But then it turned its head, the lines blurred yet again, and it took on what I believe to be its truest form.

Eyeless, soulless, gaunt and tinged with blood, its odious skin and marsh-nest hair were still not the worst thing about it. The creature raised its hands, the strings of marionettes held in its long-clawed fingers. The puppets were facsimiles of the three girls from the photo Rachel had shown me: Meghan, Joan, Piper. The strings jumped. The Joan-puppet offered the Meghan-puppet a vial of smoking liquid. The Meagan-puppet drank, fell limp. Joan tossed a noose around Meghan's neck. The creature yanked the string. The Meghan-puppet hanged. I gasped. Rachel, watching the same drama unfold, cried out.

I-G-R-A-N-T-R-E-V-E-N-G-E-F-O-R-T-H-E-O-N-E-W-H-O-D-E-S-I-R-E-S-I-T-M-O-S-T

A horrible shriek sounded inside my head. I looked to the window again. The vengeful siren opened its mouth, so wide I felt my sanity cleave from my soul. Inside its mouth was the bloody, beating heart of the last who had sought her aid, yet whose desire for revenge had been trumped by another.

W-H-Y-H-A-V-E-Y-O-U-S-U-M-M-O-N-E-D-M-E

"I want revenge," Rachel said. "I want revenge against the girl who killed my sister." I begged Rachel to think about what she was saying. "You saw what that thing can do!" I pleaded. "She's no saint. She is a witch, a charlatan, and she'll bring you to your ruin."

The thing at the window brought its hands up and hissed. It drew one filthy claw across the tops of the strings and the three marionettes, one with a gaping hole in its chest where its heart should have been, fell away.

R-E-M-E-M-B-E-R-
I-G-R-A-N-T-R-E-V-E-N-G-E-F-O-R-T-H-E-O-N-E-W-H-O-
D-E-S-I-R-E-S-I-T-M-O-S-T

For one torturous moment the shriek in my head grew louder. Then, as if someone had pressed mute, the shrieking stopped. The view beyond the window was clear. The planchette lay on its side, motionless.

We didn't talk much after that. I tried to ask Rachel how she was going to feel if some horrible fate befell her sister's friend, but she refused to discuss it, so I let it go. I suddenly felt very tired and wanted to leave more than I had at any other point in the evening. Something was nagging me—something is nagging me, even now—nibbling at the corners of my mind, something I'm certain is essential to take care of.

The drive back to the hotel was a blur. Rachel and I said goodbye, and she thanked me, though for what, I'm not sure. I asked her if she thought that thing was going to avenge her sister's death. Her response left me worried, but not for Meghan's traitorous friend:

"'I grant revenge for the one who desires it most,'" she said. "That's what the board spelled out, remember? I can't imagine that that wouldn't mean me."

On the way into the hotel, checking my pocket to ensure I had my room key, I realized that I'd somehow left the Martin residence with Helena's brooch in my possession. It occurred to me, upon looking out my window at the nearly full moon, how strange it was that I am on the other side of the Atlantic, yet the detestable Larry Brockmeyer, abuser and fugitive from justice, sleeps peacefully beneath the same thatched roof.
I think I'll go and pay him a visit.

From: Inspector Valerie Stringer
inspvalerie_stringer@kent.police.uk.com
Date: Sat, May 10, 2008 at 9:45 AM
Subject: Pending Investigation
To: Kerri Kusa kerrik0917@gmail.com

Dear Ms. Kusa,
We are writing to let you know that any contact from this point forward between you and Ms. Kimberly Fairhurst could be used as evidence in the Kent Police Department's impending investigation. If you have information as to the whereabouts of

Ms. Fairhurst, or her motive in the actions taken against Mr. Lawrence Brockmeyer, please call us at +44 1622 640730.

Thank you,
Inspector Valerie Stringer

Postscript: Ms. Fairhurst addressed a note to you on a piece of hotel stationary, which is how we came across your name. It stated that Ms. Fairhurst still 'felt bad' about your having missed out on a job opportunity given to a Mr. Brent Young. There was a black jeweled brooch atop the note. She said she wanted you to have it.

THE AFTER, PART II

by Ayesha Ahmad
artwork by Andy Fairhurst

I had promised that I would join them as soon as I was able to. I don't know how long they would have waited for me. Maybe a few days; maybe even a week. But surely no more than that – their supplies were not enough to last them longer than a week.

Part of me was resentful at that thought – that they would just leave me behind – after all, I did save their lives. But that was the irrational part. The rational part of me knew that waiting for me would have gotten them killed. I couldn't have kept them safe. I would have had to watch them night and day to make sure that the undead didn't attack them.

I had stayed back to figure out how I controlled the undead. But a couple of months later and I was no closer to finding the answer to that question. No matter what I tried or how hard I focused or meditated, I couldn't get across whatever barrier there was between the undead and me. Maybe it had been the adrenaline at the time, that had allowed me to feel their life force. Without that urgency, the panic and the desperate need to just do something, it seemed impossible to reach across the barrier and command them.

I was not accomplishing anything in this city. For lack of better options and for the pragmatic need to find food, I decided to move. The past few months I had scoured the city – there was nothing here for me. Maybe it was time to return to something marginally familiar. I never wanted to return to Islamabad – where I had seen my family die and turn into monsters.

I turned instead toward Lahore. After a few false starts and wrong directions, I finally waded through the gallis and streets and found myself on a large thoroughfare that was once the N5 national highway. I must admit, I'm shit at directions – you would think three years after society went to hell and me living on the road – I'd have developed a sense of direction – but nope. Even once I reached the highway, I spent about a day going the wrong way. Maybe if my 'honour guard' had stayed with me, they might have given me some clue as to the direction of travel. They followed me a short way out of Multan and stopped suddenly as if they had reached the end of their tether. On the outskirts of the city I stopped at an old settlement and found a serviceable bicycle and made my way down the highway.

I was glad to leave Multan with its hordes of undead. There were very few undead on the highway – I guess people near death have no desire to travel far and the undead have shown very little inclination to move too far from where they are.

I spent the days cycling down the road and the nights sheltered in crumbling buildings that used to be roadside dhabas and petrol stations. I would occasionally see a lone undead loitering about in the nearby fields or a couple at some of the dhabas. I tried connecting with them, but they ignored me as if I didn't even exist.

The road and its sameness were getting to me. Even without a single undead in sight, it wasn't simply an empty road on a late night of a public holiday when everyone is asleep at home and there are no traffic or people on the road. There were no cars to wear down the roads, but nature did the job just as well or even better. What would have been small holes or cracks had widened because of the rain or flooding. Trees had fallen.

Caked mud from overflown rivers in the past. Crumbling rocks. It was slow going. The route that would have taken barely two or three hours, was now a trek of weeks. Still I preferred the cracked and crumbling road to the wilderness growing at the edges.

I was close to Lahore now. Another roadside dhaba. An unremarkable sunny day, with blue skies, overgrown green fields, grey crumbling road, and a brown building with bits of muddied red, purple and yellow flapping on decaying undead.

Another roadside disintegrating building, with undead surrounding it in an anxious manner. Only one reason for such an accumulation of undead – humans inside. I stopped to consider the situation. I could get through the undead and to the living; but how would I get the living out? I wouldn't. I couldn't. I would just rush them to a quicker death than the one they were destined to anyway. I wonder if death by starvation would be worse than being eaten? The process of dying would be torturous no matter what. But what about death itself? I wonder if it is painful? I hope not.

As I got closer, I noticed odd details about the dead – a near skeleton covered in voluminous clothes – in life this one was huge – in death, melted flesh barely sticking to sinews and bones. A tattered burka – intact on one side and barely covering anything on the other – no modesty in death. A small figure in a scrap of red. I hope to become the undead is not painful. I wonder what it feels like to be the undead.

And by considering that question – and by considering that the undead were not simply grotesquely animated corpses; rather they felt something – I could feel the tenuous link I had with the undead. I opened a path.

And then all too suddenly I was somewhere else. I was

someone else, and I was in immense pain. Horrible, torturous unimaginable pain. Everything around me was bleak, dark, dead. I was trapped, and I was screaming. Screaming so loud that the darkness should have echoed with my agony. But I was trapped in the dark, in a cage from which not even a whisper escaped. How was it possible that no one could hear me? That no one could feel my agony. So much of it was pouring out of me that there was no room for anything else – not who I was, not my humanity. Nothing but agonizing death.

And just when it seemed that I could bear it no more, just when I was sure I was mad, just when I was about to lose myself – I was back. I was me again. The sun was shining, the birds chirping, the undead moaning, the humans screaming. Everything was as it was – just shifted sideways. A woman with long flowing hair escaping her burka, a big handsome man with a full beard, a child in a bright red sweater.

I must have fallen. I should have gotten up. I should have tried to do something for those poor humans. But it was too late. It was always too late. They were already dead. Trapped. Undead. It was too much to take in. I scrambled away, the undead's silent accusations following me.

The rest of the journey to Lahore was a blur. Why did I even bother to continue? My feet moved of their own violation. My mind hiding. Whimpering in a corner of my brain.

I became aware of the outside world on a familiar road. In the Before I had lived in this city for a couple of years. It was heartbreakingly easy to imagine what it used to look like, what it sounded like, what it felt like. I closed my eyes and slowly reconstructed in my head what was once the busy Main Boulevard road in Lahore. I imagined the people, the cars, the sounds, the honking of horns, the smell of the busy road on a balmy day. I thought of the cop directing the traffic, the people crossing the road. I thought of all those men recklessly driving their motorcycles in and out of the traffic. And I thought of me. Driving down this road for I don't know what reason. Impatient with the traffic. Cursing the guy who cut me off. Looking outside the window and seeing the buildings alongside the road. Imagining that I was heading home. It was all so real. I could almost grasp it in my hands. I could almost hear the roar of the traffic. And then it was gone.

I reluctantly opened my eyes to a world destroyed. The overgrown shrubbery, the cracks in the road, the crashed and rusted cars, the crumbling buildings. And nothing could be as it was. So, what did all this mean? And why me? Dear God. Why me? This was not simply an empty world, this was qayamat and the undead were in eternal suffering. Was this my personal hell – to be alive amongst the dead?

I moved through the city and remembered the Before. Remembering my home, remembering the people. For so long I avoided the painful memories. I thought of the people – as I knew them in the Before. The people I loved. My parents in Islamabad, who would never again call me and advise to eat well. My brother, studying in the U.K. When did he turn? We lost contact with the outside world and my parents were frantic in trying to reach before they succumbed and turned on me. Running out of the city – abandoning my cousins who were too sick to move. All my friends, coworkers, the people in the street, the children on the corner. All suffering this qayamat. My heart could not contain the pain of this shifted reality. I thought I knew grief before but now it was beyond comprehension.

Much later. I rebuilt my walls. The Before and the Turning were too painful. Focus on the here and now. There had to be more to this. There had to be a reason. Despite everything, I still believed in God. I had to. I had nothing else to hold on to. And if I believed in God, then I believed that there was a reason for this qayamat and my role in this.

I was alive and untouched for a purpose. For some reason. For my sanity's sake, I held onto this. But what exactly was this purpose? One way to find out. I was consciously blocking the undead – it was getting tiresome, it would be so easy to go down the path. But if I opened myself once again, I felt I would die – or I would understand. Either option seemed okay to me. Maybe I would have preferred to die.

I left myself open and felt the undead's trapped humanity, its anguish filled desire wash over me and for an instant, an eternity, all time, all things were irrelevant, and a dark wave overcame me and I felt like I was nowhere. All around me was a dark nothingness, a place where no light would ever enter and wave after wave of anguish and despair kept crashing into me. And beneath each wave was a whisper – a desperate whisper, trembling and exhausted and battered beyond repair – set me free. And I finally understood what they had been trying to tell me all along. The souls who were once human, but now cursed to walk the earth as the undead – the souls – the essence of humanity of what was once a living breathing person – were trapped inside the corrupted decaying bodies. These bodies with such hunger that drove them to be the most horrific of monsters. They were trapped and suffering. And they wanted me to help set them free. I was the only one that heard them.

WINDOWPANE

by Dean Kuhta
artwork by Michael Brack

Abigail peered beyond the windowpane and found loneliness.

Through the pouring rain, the street below her Victorian townhouse bustled with activity and motion. People thrust their umbrellas up against the deluge, while cars, buses, and scooters advanced through the city traffic. The occasional ring of a cable car sang in the distance.

The energetic scene may as well have been located on a distant planet. For Abigail Somberlain, confined to her home at the close of each school day, was not permitted to experience such a socially interactive and precarious environment.

"Abigail," said her mother from downstairs. "What are you doing up there? Is everything alright?"

The girl glanced at her bedroom door. It had been left open a crack, so her progress could be monitored.

"I'm fine," she replied.

"I haven't heard your violin for a while," exclaimed her mother. "What have you been doing?"

"Nothing," responded Abigail. "I'm just taking a break."

"No, ma'am. You may have a break once your lesson is complete. After that, I need you to help me with a few chores."

Abigail sighed and turned back to the dripping window. The constant hum of rain pelted against the gabled roofing and ivy-covered brick. The unbroken loneliness battered her soul.

She glanced down at her watch. It was 5:23 p.m. The tall man, Indiana, with the fedora and leather satchel bag, would be crossing Spruce Street soon. If he had a different umbrella today, however, she wondered if she would be able to recognize him.

Abigail blinked as she watched patiently for its gray and black stripes. There he was. Right on time, hopping over the puddles and back onto the sidewalk on Washington Street. The worn shoulder bag bounced against his raincoat.

"Hey there, Indiana," she whispered.

She peered down at the other end of the street for the old woman. Chloe, Abigail had named her, usually had a dark-blue handbag in one arm and her walking cane in the other. No doubt the bag would be replaced by an umbrella of her own.

The rain continued. Abigail watched.

At 5:33 p.m. Chloe emerged from a group of pedestrians crossing the intersection of Locust and Washington. To Abigail's dismay, the old woman carried no umbrella. She had instead elected to battle the elements with a wide-rimmed petal hat. A gray floral arrangement accentuated its satin sweatband. What a tough woman she was. Day after day she climbed that hill.

"Hello, Chloe."

Abigail turned her gaze back up toward Spruce. She had to spot her third and final friend before she resumed her lesson. Luca, she called him, was a young man that wore a black jacket and sputtered along on a vintage Vespa. At 5:51 p.m., the pop of its motor turned the corner and barreled down Locust Street.

"See you tomorrow, Luca," she said with a small wave.

Indiana. Chloe. Luca.

Abigail had said hello to her three friends for the day. Nevertheless, the loneliness settled back in. Like always.

"If I don't hear you practicing that violin within the next ten seconds, you are going to be in big trouble, young lady."

"I am, mother," replied Abigail.

She retreated from the window and continued her lesson.

***

"Have a good evening, Abigail," said the bus driver as the double doors opened. "Get home safe now."

"I will, Mrs. Stanley," she replied. "Goodbye."

Abigail shouldered her backpack and began the short walk home. The afternoon sun beamed bright, and the sky was a crisp blue. During the summer months in San Francisco, this usually meant that a blanket of thick fog would soon roll in from the Pacific. Sure enough, as Abigail shielded her eyes and gazed down Washington Street, she could see the mist's gray fingers clawing over the outer neighborhoods.

With a turn of a key, she stepped through the front door of her townhouse and resumed her daily isolation. Abigail stood in the foyer and stared down the darkened hallway. A singular ray of light passed through the sheer curtains of the far window and fell upon the hardwood. The combination of soft light and vivid shadow created an overwhelming sadness within her.

A hand-written note, taped to the mirror, greeted her once she finally turned and dropped the keys in a bowl on the hallway table.

"Abigail- Before you begin your homework and violin practice for the day, I need you to sweep and dust the upstairs hallway. Don't forget to vacuum the rugs this time. Also, tidy up the guest bedroom and your own room. Your dolls are all over the place. Don't worry about your sister's room. Dinner is in the fridge. Please do not go outside, under any circumstances. I'll be home no later than eight. -Mom"

The floorboards creaked and moaned as Abigail climbed the stairs. She would skip dinner again tonight. Her stomach was just not up to it.

At the second floor, Abigail paused at her younger sister's bedroom door. A bracket and four-digit padlock had been installed so that no one could enter the room. Only her mother knew the combination, and she changed it once a week.

She stared at the lock and remembered...

***

"Abigail," said her teacher. "Would you please report to the main office. Your mother would like to speak with you."

"Yes, ma'am," she replied.

The expression on her face, and tone of the teacher's voice caused Abigail's stomach to rise into her throat. This was not going to be good.

"Please have a seat, my dear," said the office secretary.

"What's wrong?" asked Abigail.

The woman gave her an awkward smile and said nothing.

Was she in trouble for something? Had they finally found out about the box of colored pencils she had taken from her art class? She cycled through every possible scenario that might cause her mother to leave work to speak with her.

The office door opened, and her mother stormed in. Her face was suffused with grief and anguish. She looked broken.

"Oh, honey," she moaned. "Candace was in an accident."

The image of her sister's face filled her mind as Abigail collapsed into her mother's arms. The darkness engulfed her.

Abigail blinked away the memory and turned from her sister's bedroom door. She entered her own room and placed the violin next to her bed. Dolls all over the place? Whatever. There was only one that she had left on the floor. All the others were aligned neatly along the shelves of the two bookcases like they always were.

"Moonchild, where did you run off to?" she said as she tossed her backpack onto the desk.

A gray and brown teddy bear sat on the windowsill. The late-afternoon sunlight accentuated the doll's tattered fur and black eyes. The stitched remnants of a silver moon were barely visible along its left breast.

"Trying to find our friends before I do?"

She picked up the bear and gently stroked a patch of its muddled fabric. Her recent repairs were not very impressive. The threads below the left leg were unraveling, and stuffing protruded from the hole that once contained the right arm.

"I know you're a mess," she replied. "I've tried to patch you up, but none of the other dolls want to give up one of their arms. Can you blame them?"

Moonchild's lifeless eyes stared back at her.

"What?" she exclaimed and shook her head. "No, ma'am. You know that's not possible. We're not allowed to go into her room, and I don't even know if he's in there anyway. Besides, what makes you think he'd want to give up his arm?"

Abigail lightly twisted one of the bear's small eyes.

"How are these things always coming loose? What do you do all day while I'm at school?"

The bear remained silent.

"Yea, you wish," she answered. "I don't believe a word of

your make-believe stories, and you'd better stop talking about Candace's room. Otherwise, you're going to go right back up on that bookshelf with all the others. Is that what you want?"

She placed Moonchild back on the windowsill.

"Look what time it is. We don't want to miss saying hello to our friends, do we?"

A commuter bus thundered down Washington as Abigail looked through the windowpane. Whispers of silky fog began to swirl along the rooftops and down the streets. The late-afternoon sun faded into a curious restlessness.

"There's Indiana," said the girl. "And look, Moonchild, he's wearing his hat today. Wave hello."

She moved the bear's remaining arm to simulate a wave.

"Time for Chloe. I bet you she has her blue handbag this time. Here she comes, conquering that old hill like always."

A sudden clamor emanated from the hallway outside her door. Abigail turned her head at the sound, at the same time struggling to keep her attention on the street. She did not want to miss Luca. A moment later, the Vespa's sputtering engine turned the corner. She spun back to the window with a frown.

"Hey there, Luca. See you tomorrow."

Abigail sighed and turned to face her open door. She stared into the shadowy hallway and felt the familiar feelings saturate her mind. Loneliness. Despair. Sorrow. They borrowed their claws deep within her consciousness. The daily ritual with her inaccessible friends had come and gone in an instant, and the bleak reality of her life had returned. She stood and walked into the hallway to begin her chores.

***

"Good night, Abigail," said the bus driver.

"Bye, Mrs. Stanley," she replied. "See you tomorrow."

The fog had already enveloped the city streets as Abigail opened her front door. She placed her keys in the bowl and then stared down the hallway at the light. It was dimmer today, but still exuded a paralyzing melancholy. She stared in awe.

Abigail hung up her jacket after a few quiet moments and then peeled her mother's note from the mirror.

"Abigail- Since today is Thursday, I need you to wipe down the kitchen counters and take the trash bags out to the back. There are five of them this week, so you'll have to make two trips, but don't go beyond the back porch. Continue reading your book for at least an hour and then work on your violin lesson. Your first recital is coming up next month, so you need to be ready. Also, you know better than to go into your sister's room. The door was left wide open. Why would you do such a thing? Dinner is in the fridge. I'll be home by nine tonight. -Mom"

She stared at the piece of paper with confusion and dread. A sudden light-headedness overwhelmed her as she felt the hairs on her neck stand on end.

Candace's door had been left open? But how? She had not done it. She did not even know the current password.

Abigail placed her mother's note back on the foyer table and then slowly lifted her gaze to the stairwell. At the top step loomed impenetrable darkness. It was utterly devoid of light or form. Or was it? She focused her eyes into the black.

A faint glow gracefully emerged from the shadows. The delicate lines and curves of a female silhouette stepped forward.

"Abi," it whispered.

Abigail expelled a panicked breath and fell back to the hardwood. She kicked her feet forward as she hit the floor and desperately tried to push herself back along the hallway. Away from the vision and away from the cold whisper. A whisper that could only have been uttered by one person.

Her dead sister.

Candace.

***

Abigail raised her head and moaned. Why was she lying on the floor in the downstairs hallway? What had happened? What time was it?

Her entire body was sore. The bones in her neck popped as she looked down at her watch. It was 5:19 p.m.

Her friends! She could not miss them.

Abigail painfully lifted herself to a standing position and rubbed her forehead. Why were her muscles aching so much? Had she fallen down the stairs? She could not remember. Her mind felt sluggish and lethargic. A distant memory tickled the back of her mind as she struggled to regain her thoughts. The nebulous image of her sister's face intermingled with her friends from the windowpane.

"I need to get to the window."

She held tight to the railing and ascended the stairwell. A sudden chill overcame her as she passed her sister's door. Abigail resisted the curious sensation and rushed to her room.

A torrent of fog rolled along the street.

"No," she cried. "I can't see anyone!"

She checked her watch. 5:23 p.m. had come and gone.

"Indiana, please don't go."

Through the gloom, Abigail could just make out the dress shoes and high heels of the commuters as they bustled along the concrete. Their identities, however, were completely obscured. The Vespa's motor chugged down Washington Street.

"Luca, I can't see you."

Abigail began to cry into her hands and then thought of the old woman, Chloe. She had been out of turn.

The girl slowly raised her eyes back to the window and felt a breath of terror escape from her lips.

Through a break in the fog, Chloe stood stock-still on the sidewalk and stared up at Abigail. The eerie expression on the old woman's face radiated an overwhelming sense of dread. Chloe raised her right hand and held up four fingers.

Then three.

Then all five.

She raised her left hand and displayed seven.

Four. Three. Five. Seven.

The old woman shook her head, as if recovering from a profound daydream. The fog devoured her, and she disappeared.

Abigail was in shock. What had she just seen? Why had Chloe stared right at her and held up her fingers?

"The lock," whispered a soft voice.

The girl looked down at Moonchild. The bear blinked its eyes and smiled.

"Holy shit," exclaimed Abigail. "What the…?"

"Chloe just showed you the code for Candace's room."

"You're talking to me. You don't really talk."

"Clearly, I can," replied the bear. "So, are you going to go into her room again, or not?"

"Again? I haven't been in her room since she died."

"Seriously?" replied Moonchild. The bear stood up and leaned against the edge of the windowsill. "You say this every day. I wonder if you'll ever remember the things we do."

Abigail rubbed her eyes and moaned. "This isn't real. I must have hurt my head when I fell down the stairs."

"Oh, it's very real. And you didn't just fall down the stairs. Candace summoned you and then you fainted. She wants to speak with you in her room again."

"I've gone crazy," said Abigail.

"No, you haven't," replied Moonchild. "Quit being so melodramatic and go on. She's waiting for you."

The girl stood in the middle of the room in a daze. The past twelve months had become a waking nightmare. Since the death of her sister, the daily routine had been filled with unending anguish, loss, and solitude. Not only did her mother prevent her from ever leaving the confines of their home, but strange visions and sensations had materialized. The bizarre light in the downstairs hallway. The coldness as she passed her sister's door. These haunting impressions had transferred their grief into the two aspects of her life that she cherished most. Her friends through the windowpane, and her bear Moonchild.

"I can't go on like this," she said.

"You're right," replied the bear.

Abigail took a deep breath. She left her room and stood before her sister's door. The combination lock waited for her.

Four. Three. Five. Seven. Enter.

An electronic ding emitted from the device and the lock clinked open. The girl pushed open the door and entered the room. A brilliant, warm glow engulfed her mind and body, and she willingly submitted to its heavenly grasp.

***

"Abi," said Candace. "Let's go back to your room. We don't want to miss saying hello to all our friends, do we?

"In a second," replied Abigail. "I can't find that one doll of yours. Where did you leave it?"

"The bear?"

"Yes."

"She's called Moonchild. Check under my desk."

"Here it is," said Abigail as she retrieved the bear by its right arm. "Didn't Mom get this for your birthday? Why don't you like it?"

"She did, and I do like it very much," answered Candace. "But I thought I'd give it to you."

Abigail looked at the bear lovingly.

"Thank you, but why?"

Candace smiled. "See the silver moon I stitched onto her? My bear, Sunchild, has a little sun on his chest and I thought that they could be best friends. Like us. Plus, you don't have any dolls of your own."

"I love it," she said. "Why did you name it Moonchild?"

"Because of her powers. She can fly in the moonlight and my bear can fly in the sunlight. And when they are together, they can do all kinds of neat, magical stuff."

"Wow, I wish I had your imagination."

"Follow me to the windowpane," said Candace. "And I'll show you how we can create some new characters from the people on the street. Then we can go outside and play with our dolls. Would you like to do that?"

"More than anything," replied Abigail.

Follow Abigail Somberlain's further adventures in:
Silvarum, Book I: Frost

PATHFINDER

by Jake Bauer

artwork by Andy Fairhurst

An expansive vista sprawled below me. I overlooked a verdant valley, perched precariously in the midst of a tree's boughs, and scanned the distant tree tops, waiting for the sign. A distant wind made the forest below me ripple like waves in a lake or like a green blanket being cast over a bed, but still I was vigilant. The sun was just cresting the mountain peaks to the South when I saw it: a faint red haze snaking through the trees, about half a kilometer below me deep in the valley. It stopped, and I knew now was my time to strike.

This particular quarry always had to rest after a hunt and transforming was a painful and drawn out process, meaning now was the time. I carefully descended and checked that my gear was in order. I strapped on my black steel blade (I called my sword Yrhael, which meant Northern Wind in our language), checked my brace of throwing knives, and made double sure the straps on my amp gauntlet were tight. A simple three step process I repeated ere every hunt, as I found it helped clear my head.

Content that I was all set to go, I snuffed my small cookfire and set off down the gradient into the valley, eyes and ears on high alert. I followed the red mist and as it grew sharper and sharper, my movements became more and more stealthy. Some of the beast's enhanced senses were still in effect even during the reverting process.

Finally, with the sun now almost directly overhead, I reached the edge of the clearing the monster had chosen to become human again, and with a flash, the whole situation became clear: the people of the village had difficulty tracking this werewolf because it was one of them. A boy of fourteen or fifteen, whom I recognized immediately. I thought it odd. These were hardy frontier folk, well used to protecting their homes from any manner of beast or creature of ill intent.

The boy was naked, lying supine on the forest floor, his body was still patchy with fur in spots and his head was still awfully distorted, nose and muzzle a terrible collage of human and wolf. The fact that he was still this distinctly wolfish so far into the daylight was a bad sign. Every Pathfinder knew it got harder and harder to reclaim one's humanity the longer one rampaged as a wolf.

I drew my sword, and as I entered the clearing, I wondered briefly if the boy was conscious of his actions. If he was (for whatever reason in his head) actively in control of himself while he was taken over by Moonrage. His still pointed ears perked up and a deep growl emanated from his chest. They always fought to stay alive, a base animal in all of us.

The werewolf staggered to its feet and met my gaze, and for a brief instant I thought I saw a flicker of remorse, which always seemed to happen in these situations. Then, powered by rage or hunger or some other deeper and darker impetus, he lunged at me. His right arm was still viciously clawed and furry, but his left arm was almost completely human again. So that's where I struck. Deftly moving into his swipe, I followed through with an upward slash, lopping off the human arm just below the shoulder. The wolf stumbled forward, his blackish-red blood seeping into the loam beneath the grass, and he howled in pain; piercing through the forest and echoing off the looming mountains. I spun and remained at the ready, Yrhael in the classic opening stance of our first sword form, ready for another lunge. The wolf was wobbly as it lurched around to face me once more, any flash of humanity long gone from its eyes. It bared its fangs and raised its wolf-arm to strike - and in that moment where his hand just crested the apex of the swipe; I lunged with a wicked thrust of my own. With a dull thunk, I drove forward, forcing the tip of my sword deeper through its heart until it emerged from the beast's back. It emitted a final gurgling growl and went limp on my sword and died. I let it fall off Yrhael and sheathed her not bothering to wipe off the blood. Blacksteel was always thirsty. I heaved a sigh and drew my field dagger, kneeling just at the wolf's neck. There was always one more step to ending a cursed beast once and for all.

I left the village a scant two days later. A missive from Ird Fortress bade me move on to the next hunt, just enough time to display the head of the man-wolf, tell the townspeople the situation, and get some rest at the small inn in the village.

As I walked the western road out of the village, I read the missive. It said:

"Surrand village, north west, investigate."

In my years of ranging one thing had almost always run true - the shorter the briefing the higher the risk of harm. This was the shortest one I had received in quite some time, and my neck hairs stood in anticipation. Surrand village was a day's march away, according to my map of the region, and about the same size as the village I was leaving, maybe a bit bigger. If anything, it was less remote, closer to the warmer clines further north and the second to last stop of the Road of the Emperor, approximately three days from the capital city, Miranda. I wondered as I walked, what exactly could be terrorizing a place that, if not well guarded, had at least some military presence?

The missive wasn't talking, so it was up to me. I pondered on who would be my contact out here in the sticks. Surrand had no Pathfinder Hall, but our order hunts for whoever needs it, so we had what we called middlemen positioned in every established settlement.

Surrand... Surrand...

Then it clicked, the middleman for Surrand also oversaw the village further south along the Road (a place called Heregorn and the end of the Road in question). She was the village apothecary, and long had she kept watch for us Pathfinders out in the Phalanx foothills. Route set in my mind, so I buckled down for the day's walk. It turned out to be uneventful. Every hour or so a cart would pass, merchants and farmers looking to ply their trade. Nothing like the glamour of the markets and traders in Miranda, these were simpler matters: blacksmithing apprentices offering tool repairs and carting around anvils and small forges, furriers with covered carts smelling of animals and must; and farmers with baskets, crates and bushels of produce and fruit.

The Phalanx was a veritable pantry, and fed most of the kingdom, especially now in the height of summer when fields and orchards were heavy with their bounties and the forests teemed with life. The sun was already past its zenith for the day, and the mid-afternoon was pleasantly warm for the southern foothills. It would get cooler when night fell. The Twin Ladies soared across the sky in an endless waltz among uncountable stars.

As the sun inched closer to the eastern horizon, I crested a final hill and saw the village of Surrand in the distance. It was surrounded by a wooden palisade. Watchmen patrolled the perimeter with torches and crossbows. Thankfully, the village's gates were not yet sealed for the night. Besides, they would certainly let me in, monsters be damned. Pathfinders had that sort of privilege in the Kingdom, as evidenced by the occasional respectful nod I often received, even here on the fringes of the realm, when one spied my kit or my heavily tattooed left arm. Not only were the tattoos different among Pathfinders, they were granted upon merit on mission completion or significant milestone reached, but each one was imbued with ancient (and little understood) magic. They granted us trademark abilities like monster tracking sight, night-vision, or enhanced speed and reflexes. They also allowed us to tap into the Ley Lines to use our brand of mysticism. These were split into two schools with vastly different outcomes based on which school one was more attuned to. This, in turn, was based on which arm a Pathfinder could most efficiently channel Ley force through. There was the Martial school, channeled through the left arm, members of which were immediately trained as Rangers, and the Mystic school, which resided in the Ird Fortress studying their books and scrolls channeling through the right. Rangers were the muscle, the mercenaries, the face of the order. The Scholars were the brains.

The tattoos were a badge unlike any other. Permanent twisting knotworks and arcane symbols. Faces from the past and deities, etched into my very skin, each one a hunt or a story; and each one imbuing me with more abilities. As I approached the gate with nightfall rapidly approaching and stars already popping up in the indigo sky, one look at my arm and the gate swung open, almost without a word. I sat at a well-worn table that appeared to be hewn from the stump of a massive oak tree. Years and years of countless patrons' scratch marks, drink rings, and various wearing downs colored the tabletop like a map of some faraway continent. The light inside the tavern was dim, lit only by a few guttering oil lanterns and a merrily crackling fire in the stone hearth at the far end of the room. Oddly, it was also quiet this evening. Typically, after a long day's work in the fields or behind the counter, folks out here almost always wound down with a mug of ale and a plate of stew.

The middleman sat across from me, a woman who took age as gracefully as possible. Her auburn hair streaked with silver, and the barest hint of wrinkling showed at the corners of her eyes. She still wore her apothecary's apron, stuffed with phials and small bottles filled with tinctures and powders, and sachets of herbs and other substances. Everything to ply her trade and, in her words, she never left home without it. She was built like a person accustomed to long walks in harsh territories, and her hands were callused and scarred almost as much as my own.

She was the true image of the independent frontiers woman. Her name was Evelyn, but she preferred Eve. As she described the situation to me, hunched over the table, voice low like we were conspiring against the crown, her tale became more and more grim. I sipped my ale and listened intently.

She explained that it had all started about a month ago, when the Cooper's son went foraging for summer berries and never returned home. No one worried on the first night, often children and young people camped overnight rather than risk walking in the dark, but when the third night arrived, the panic began to set in. A search party was organized, but no trace of the boy was found. The only evidence discovered was his half-filled basket of strawberries and currants, tossed amongst the bushes. On the fifth day, the Farrier's daughter vanished from her home.

One night, the family went to bed then the next day she was simply gone. Nothing was disturbed except the girl's bedclothes. Things continued like this until my arrival. Parents weren't sleeping, the town watch had tripled, and the gate stayed closed firmly from the first hint of dusk 'till the sun was fully in the sky. Still, children kept disappearing every three to four days for a total of about ten children just gone. The town watch reported foul shadows shifting in the trees just beyond the range of their torches, and things that had made the trees rustle as they moved past them in the forest.

She must have seen the grimness on my face.

"Is it bad, Havardir?" she asked.

I paused, thinking, mid sip. I set my mug down and swallowed. "It could be, yes. I'm going to the wall, feel free to join me."

I left a coin on the table as I stood and left, my mind racing. Eve followed, a new grimness on her face. I had dealt with things like this before; there was much power in the blood of innocents. The detail that struck me about all this was that apparently there was no trace. People and beasts always left traces.

Villagers eyed me fearfully from their windows, drawing the curtains, knowing that any night they could be the next victims, Pathfinder or no. We reached the wall and ascended the tight zig-zag stairwell to the top of the gate, meeting up with the guard captain. He was a man with a weathered face and salt and pepper hair visible underneath his helmet. A few days' worth of stubble covered his face and he met my gaze with hardened eyes that then drifted to my arm and filled with understanding. Relief passed over his face and, wordlessly, he gestured out to the darkness. I stepped to the edge of the heavily reinforced palisade and gazed out to the darkness. Indeed, my eyes picked up on the movement of the shadows and a faint red mist weaved in and out from behind the trees. The thing that gave me pause was the size of it. The mist surrounded the village with no gaps. Here and there, as if probing, the mist extended then withdrew from torchlight or some other unknown thing.

Then, as I looked, the whispering started. Faint at first, rising and falling with the breeze, but then becoming clearer and clearer. Almost as if it knew I could hear it, the mist suddenly and violently coalesced into one shape directly ahead, which then split into two distinct shapes, one of which began to approach the gate, while the other retreated and vanished. I looked around at my companions. They were unaware of what had just happened.

I met the eyes of the guard captain, and he read in them what I was about to say. "Ready your men, and tell them not to hit me. Something approaches."

I ran back down the staircase and quickly unslung my stowed kit and removed the weight of my living utensils. I slipped on my mail hauberk, pulled over it my leather tabard and then belted on Yrhael and my knives. I pulled my Amp Gauntlet over my left and flexed my fingers to ensure no empty space, then buckled it to my forearm as tight as it would go.

Steeling myself, I pushed open the gate (which was quickly pulled closed again and barred behind me) and walked to face whatever was coming. The first thing I noticed was the silence of it, followed quickly by the size. The beast towered over the average man, standing nearly twenty feet, almost eye level with the top of the gate. As it entered the light, its appearance became known. Cries and shouts echoed from the wall and I drew Yrhael, breath quickening. It was hideous, unlike anything I'd ever seen after nearly fifteen years ranging. Its skin was a deathly green-blue color, and pupil-less eyes fiery with intelligence glowed yellow. There was no mouth or nose to speak of. Instead, tendrils extended like a beard to its chest. It had the vague shape of a man, but ruthlessly distorted. The right arm was replaced with a massive tentacle, as thick as a tree trunk, writhed and twisted. The legs ended in flattened stumps. It was man and squid and tree and terror formed into one being.

I felt ice in my blood, then stifled it. Now was not the time for fear. I flexed my fingers, forming the spell, and cast a simple Arrow at the beast. I charged forward after releasing the missile, sword raised. The bolt hit the creature and erupted in a shower of sparks. The beast's skin took the brunt of the blow and was barely singed, a tiny hole where the Arrow had struck. I reached it and swung a terrible downward strike with Yrhael, aiming for the trunk of its left leg. My sword pierced it, but it seemed like the monster's body simply pushed my blade out, and I withdrew in horror as the large laceration I had caused began to close itself - not fully - but the meat of the wound seemed to knit itself together like a hole in a sweater.

The monstrosity glowered down at me and I felt the air chill as it raised its tentacle arm to strike. I leapt to the right with a tuck and roll and then sprang to my feet. Yrhael was raised for a counter-strike on the tentacle. I used all my momentum but ended up only halfway through cutting it off, then the same thing happened with its leg. The tentacle began to repair itself before my eyes. I realized that the beast had been completely silent this whole time, no roar of pain or anger or hatred, just cold, calculating onslaught. I leapt again as it recovered, this time directly at it, and struck again at the still closing wound on the tentacle. Striking true, Yrhael sliced through almost all of it, but left it hanging by a thread. The arc of my jump carried me directly into its human hand and it grasped me fully and lifted me to eye level, pinning my arms to my side. It cocked its head to the side, like a child looking at a strange new toy.

I was calm, even though for all intents and purposes I was dead to rights. I slowly moved my left hand in the shape of a spell, feeling the Ley Lines power flow into my gauntlet. It was a gamble, but I was stuck. The spell was a long and complex, and I paused right before the last finger movement and looked once more into the creature's eyes. Boredom was all I saw.

I smirked and did the last finger motion, and the thing's face was engulfed in a starburst explosion of magical energy. Thankfully, it dropped me quick, and I was able to catch myself and roll away. Yrhael remained at the ready. It screamed then, as the second explosion engulfed its face, sending tendrils flying and obscuring its view. It erupted a scream somewhere between the roar of a bear and the call of a crow. Unearthly, but strangely human.

The beast stumbled forward and fell with barely a sound or any indication of its size. I immediately sprang into action and aimed another downward swing at its neck, which I felt connect through my arms. My blade got stuck again, but I wasn't giving up. I wrenched it free and brought it down, again and again, until the creature's head was severed. I stood panting above the lifeless body and watched as it started steaming. Its flesh bubbled and smoked and sloughed away, leaving behind no trace except for the corpses of the missing children. Three of them had grievous wounds to their right arms, four of them had their necks severed, and one had a gash on her leg. I sighed and walked over to the motionless forms, inspecting them. As I looked at their lifeless figures, I felt the weight and the tedium of dead things drape over my shoulders.

The gates opened, and a procession of guards filed out. Their solemn faces mixed with awe at my slaying of the monstrosity. I stood from my inspection and looked to the guard captain.

"This was not a random occurrence. Gather your dead, I will pursue the perpetrators," I said.

Without waiting for a reply, I turned and began to run into the forest, towards the other red mist that was attempting a retreat. I shaped another spell with my left hand and soon my strides grew longer. Breathing had become easier and my speed nearly doubled along with my reflexes. It was a dangerous invocation, but my anger and sadness fueled it without much concern for the drawbacks.

I closed in on the mist, feeling the dangerous boiling rage of the Berserker roiling in my stomach. I jerked to a halt as I reached the red fog. In front of me loomed a cyclopean tower. It was steadily sinking into a rift in the ground and displayed an open portcullis at its front. From the doorway sprung tendrils, glowing softly with a fell green light. There were five robed figures, one of which stepped to meet me. He spoke in a deadpan, his face was featureless and behind his eyes I could see the same unearthly glowing light peeking out from under his hood.

"You come too late. I withdraw from your wretched realm. My objective is complete, and now I know your face. Crowborn. We will meet again, and you will know death."

I lunged forward and began swinging Yrhael, cutting down the robed figures as sinister laughter rang from the tower, now almost completely submerged in the earth. I stood panting and watched it disappear, leaving no trace, surrounded by the bloodless bodies of the robed figures now cut to ribbons. I felt everything drain out of me: the spell and all of the rage I held in my heart and felt nothing but the weight of emptiness.

The village of Surrand was safe again, but at what cost? And what now? I had obviously attracted the attention of some eldritch being. It was time to return to Ird Fortress, but first a well-deserved rest back at Surrand. And explanations, of course. What I could give, at least. Sheathing Yrhael and trudging back to the village, I realized that this fight was only just beginning.

HAND OF FATE

by Victor Johnston
artwork by Brett Gray

The warehouse where I worked had just let out the day prior to my arrival on the mountainside. You see, like clockwork, my employer routinely shuts down just before the middle of December every year. Several factors cause them to make this decision; low volume of work for its employees, poor weather, and low work ethic during the holiday season. They did not like to waste our time, or their time, so they would send us all on a mandatory paid vacation.

I can still recall their faces from that last day before the shutdown. Each of my co-workers, oh so cheerily wishing their Happy Holidays to one-another, knowing we wouldn't reconvene until after the start of the new year. Well, at least amongst themselves. I spent my hours trapped there in what was once my dark office. Four sloppily painted beige walls, poly-fiber ceiling tiles, and tiny plastic five-star rated, safety glass windows had separated me from the other workers. Between all of that, and the constant buzz of machinery, not a soul recognized I was there on a normal day of operations. So, to me, it doesn't seem a stretch that anyone would go out of their way to share tidings of happiness during the most festive time of year. I just sat there and peeped out of the window from my desk as they laughed and conversed.

I had been "slaving away" in that office for a few years now, handling and inputting raw data and processing the routes of our shipments. However, most days I began to wish I would have been on the floor chucking boxes onto the backs of the trucks, as I had become a bit too portly during my tenure there. I found it somewhat difficult traversing the hillside due to this, getting short of breath on the way. I had decided this year, I would make the trip to the cabin my grandfather left for me, as a part of his final wishes. The old man could have left it to my sister with her husband and kids, but they lived four states over. Or the gift could have been bestowed to my parents, but at their age, I think they would have fared worse than I traveling here. Maybe I had been fated to receive it, or perhaps he chose me because I look like a stumpy, round lumberjack.

My breath bore itself visible in the frigid temperatures, as my legs burned during the three-mile hike to the humble abode. I passed a few other seemingly empty lodges on my way and wondered if I was the only soul out there at the time. Eventually, my walk of the trail brought to me the visage of building 2-E; a quaint, small, antiquated wood building near the end of the trail. I should have reveled in the beauty of nature a bit more on that strenuous ascent. I had not an idea of the events that were to unfurl on that accursed hillside.

Both thankfully, and to my chagrin, on the night of my arrival I located a crank powered weather radio in the tiny living area. I found it to be equipped with all the bells and whistles: a flashlight and emergency beacon. Upon charging and activating the radio, a static-marred, pre-recorded voice was calling for an evacuation of everyone on the mountain due to an incoming pop-up winter storm. I had enough supplies to last for at least four weeks if I rationed it out, so at the time, there was no immediate reason to fear being snowed in. Also, I had no fear of missing work, after-all, it's impossible to be snowed in for a month or longer. Looking back, how I wish I had stayed in the city and never come to this wretched place; regret isn't even strong enough of a word. My intentions were to visit the cabin to escape the bustle of city life for a time. However, I realize now, I would rather have slept my days away in my lonely apartment. My safe, warm, cozy apartment. That would have been a better choice, than the pointless fate I have relegated myself to.

At first the snow was beautiful, as it slowly drifted to the ground. Flakes danced about in the swirling wind within the rolling backdrop of a grey sky. However, soon the storm became so heavy, the windows themselves were obscured and blotted out the once picturesque view of mountainside around me. I assumed at first the storm would carry on for a few hours, perhaps a day at most. A foolhardy assumption, thinking all would be okay, and that it would not accumulate in abundance. However, during the first evening after I had laid myself down to rest, I was greeted by a low rumbling coming from what seemed to be all directions. It felt as if the earth was swaying and churning around me. I assumed I had fallen victim to an avalanche, but it could have all been in my head, as I am an extremely vivid dreamer. I do know afterwards I utilized my weight to push the only door ajar, but to no avail.

Thankfully there was a fireplace, albeit minuscule, and a pile of mostly dry wood in that old ramshackle shanty. I feared igniting it after I believed the chimney had become covered from the snowfall, but I would freeze to death had I not attempted to stoke a flame. I had no way of knowing the condition the wood was in as the cabin had been vacant for quite some time but assumed it would burn. Fuel is fuel, too dry or not, and there was a freezing darkness that blanketed the room I needed to warm and illuminate. The light cast from the radio was negligible to say the least, and not suited for the task of providing a lasting light.

Time passed, slow and torturous. I felt as if I was stuck in those lumber-laden walls for...I don't even know how long. Three weeks? Longer? Too many days of agonizing solitude. One would assume I had grown used to seclusion with minimal contact at work and living alone. However, I felt a different type of desolation, almost like an embodiment of solitude was there in that very cabin with me. Soon I found my sanity becoming strained, and for whatever moronic reason, I would turn the dial in a feeble attempt to hear another human voice. However, the radio seemed incapable of receiving signals any longer, perhaps a relay tower had suffered damage or lost power. With each maddening dial turn, only white noise met my query. I suppose I began to develop cabin fever and became increasingly agitated with my situation as random thoughts of life began to dart about in my mind.

Somehow, I managed to force one of the two windows open, ever so slightly. Just mere inches. This action was fruitless as the snow was packed so tight, it would prove impossible to burrow through. Even with a hatchet I located near the pile of wood, I found it would not suffice as the tool I needed. The snow had frozen into a solid wall of ice.

The initial panic began to nestle in just a bit deeper, evolving, presenting itself now as a much more sinister feeling of dread. Could the weight of the frozen snow collapse the building? What if I was wrong and it would take months for the packed snow to melt? I had to force myself back to reality from my descent into dismay, I was panicking and sweating profusely. My layering of clothes had become soaked. Despite my swirling mind, I realized I was able to at least collect paltry shavings of ice from the small crack to hydrate myself. This task was almost not worth the reward, as it expended quite a bit of energy.

The time eventually came, and the stockpile of wood had reached the final few logs at the bottom. As I stated previously, most of the logs seemed dry, except for the last one on the bottom of the pile. It seemed to have played home to some burrowing insects, as it was soft and rotten. I should have known it was the lame one of the bunch, the way the stack leaned in the direction of that piece. I was becoming increasingly cold and frustrated as the temperatures amplified, and my supplies ran low. I hadn't rationed them out very intelligently, as I assumed this ordeal would be over much sooner. Terrible mistakes sealed my fate. My terrible mistakes. I punched the log as hard as I could with a tightly clutched left fist, and the log just disintegrated due to the advancement of the rot. A small piece of the wood pierced the skin through my cheap cotton glove, as the blow went right through it, my fist meeting the floor. Dust kicked up into my eyes and lungs as well and caused me to wince and break into a coughing fit. The tears and hacking subsided after some time had passed, but I was left uneasy.

That blunder became the precursor to the depressing snowball effect that I was to suffer. First, I had to start burning what little furniture there had been within the cabin for heat. Then my food began to run critically low. Then nightmares set in, unending nightmares of decaying bodies, vile beasts, and death. Not once did I awaken feeling well rested, nor free of sweat.

Every single god forsaken moment in that hellish cabin, I could no longer tell if it was day or night. It's as if time itself was muddled together. To make matters worse, every time I was able to lull myself asleep, I was jolted awake by the feeling of a scratching, searing pain beneath my left palm. The skin was getting thinner, as if it were being scratched away and eroded from below. I began to see a revolting pulsation beneath my flesh, as the muscles were beginning to spasm in my palm. I knew I needed to take measures to alleviate the problem.

You see, my grandfather left me this straight razor before passing away. He gave it to me just before I finished my studies at university. I fashion myself something of a beard aficionado, so I've never used it once, maybe just to tighten my edges. As I elect to just grow my burly mane, the blade is as sharp as the day I last saw him. I have attempted to keep it in its refined condition.

That final back and forth I had with the old man remains etched into my memory, conjuring the image of his atrophied body lying there in that hospital bed, while I stood at his side. I thought he was attempting to beautifully cloak his gift in some sort of mystique that night.

"Skip, I ain't lookin' to stick around here much longer, right," he said as he lay in his hospital bed.

I gave a flippant rebuttal about how I didn't think he was going to be leaving that building anytime soon in his condition, to which his airy laugh met my cheeky quip. I regretted this shortly after an array of hacking and struggling to catch his breath followed. I repeatedly asked him if he was okay as he coughed away, only to be met with his bony, weather worn hand, outstretched as if to push me away. As he steadied himself, he drew in a deep phlegmy breath, and shut his eyes to put himself in a moment of reflection.

"Listen in, alright. You know good and well when I wore a younger man's clothes, I was made to take a trip to hell and back. I've told you too many stories as a boy, for you to not know that. Some of them I know your mother hates me for." His labored speech stopped for a moment as he caught his breath.

"I went over there to crush those Hanz, Franz, and Fritz boys like roaches."

His words gasped out, as his bony arm pointed in no particular direction. I stood there silently at his bedside, as he began to recount a tale he had never told another soul before. The beeps of the EKG machine at times in perfect cadence with the rise and fall of his storytelling. Supposedly, after liberating a small shantytown of vagrants and gypsies, he claimed to have happened across a trader among its residents. An aged, wild-eyed woman had talked him into perusing her wares. Just as his gaze happened across what seemed to be a German soldier's straight razor, the hag reached out to him, and made an exclamation.

"Reward! For a savior. Your kin, give this. You will know when, ready. Safety...No! A solution. It brings," the crazed woman uttered in her broken English.

As he tells it, the gypsy's stare never left his eyes, as she took his hands into hers, and deposited the treasure. He said it was almost as if a mystifying glow in her eyes had frozen him where he stood. My grandfather didn't remember slipping it into his pant pocket, but there it rested later that evening as he told his fellow soldiers about the encounter.

He said I could find the heirloom at his small estate, wrapped in newspapers in the top drawer of a workbench. The old man followed up that bit of insight, with the candid attitude I had known him to have my entire life.

"For God's sake, please get it before your money-grubbing father clears out the place. You're the only one I figured

I would trust with this story, and you would benefit from that relic the most. You're a young man, keep it on ya', you'll know when to use it." These last words cumbrously made their way past his dry lips. Almost as if telling this tale was his swan song, he sunk back into the pillow, looking mortally tired.

Those final words swirled in my head, recalling the events from that night with him. I began to revel in the shine of that cared-for blade as I flipped it open, and this helped season the madness from my itching palm so much more. The balance of the handle, the sharpness of the blade. I knew it was perfect for this job. With my teeth gnashed, I slid the sharpest point over my palm, and the warmth of fresh blood caressed my arm. Each drop nesting itself in my forearm hair before dropping to the floor. I dug into the open wound with my right hand and found what seemed to be a maggot. As I attempted the extraction, its tail broke off, and the worm retracted deeper into my palm.

The itching and burning from the creature had stopped for what I would guess to be two days. Again, I can't be sure of time. The healing process had taken over, accompanied by the burning and itching. However, once again as I tried to sleep, the scratching returned. It felt like there were more of them, all trying to remove themselves from their prison of flesh.

As I awoke the next day, I gnashed my teeth and gritted through removing more of these disgusting bugs from my palm. Nearly twenty in total. I found it difficult to look at my bloodied appendage as I removed the parasites, turning my head and digging them out based on feeling.

I vomited several times. From shock? Disgust? Blood loss? I'm sure they all played a part, but I was glad to have removed them. But I was weary. Did they retract like the first?

It felt as if an eternity had passed. Healing went much slower as opposed to the wake of the first time I had "surgically removed" these things from myself. A smell of infected flesh permeated the walls of my snow-bound prison. The last bit of my rations was now devoured, and I began to feel my body turning against me. Could I blame it? I slept less and less as I became more exhausted, and a higher degree of madness was settling in. I began to scream until my voice failed. There was nowhere for my cries to travel, except back to my own ears. Cracked, cold, bleeding lips lent to the collective unease I was engulfed by. In tears and absolute pain, I laid my head down, wrapped in blankets. I accepted the fact that I was probably going to die on that hillside.

Suddenly, from a terrible restless slumber, I was awoken by a burning and scratching through my entire arm. The pain was insurmountable. I threw the warm covers off, to be embraced by the freezing cold as I ran to the washroom with the radio in hand. In the dull light emitted by the flashlight, I could see a coursing of wriggling maggots beneath my skin, from my scarred, infected palm, to the top of my forearm. Dismay pushed my legs into a frenzy, and I ran to the front door, repeatedly crashing into it, in an attempt for a divine miracle. Clutching the pain riddled arm, I slid down with my back against the wall.

The tears flowed down my cheeks, as I realized I had to remove... No... Please not like this...

I feverishly cut and tore pieces of blanket, to tie around my bicep as the parasites writhed within my body. I could feel popping tendons, and I am sure I fractured fingers on my left hand ripping my clothes apart to do this. The poor condition of the stricken arm made it near powerless. However, those damaged digits were going to be lying on the floor with my dead arm soon, and the pain only pushed me forward to finish the grim undertaking.

The sharp shining blade pressed into the fat, sinew, and muscle of my bicep, as I cried out for some god to help me. A quick pooling of dark, thick, almost tainted blood beneath me, told me I must have hit an artery. I did not care. Death is a welcomed release from this frozen tomb and parasitical torment. I began to push the blade deeper, as my screams were thrown back to me by the cabin walls, taunting me. I began to rock the blade to-and-fro. Harder, faster, circling the whole of my arm. As I cut deeper, my sweat, blood, and tears matted my hair to my face. A dizzy queasiness enveloped me. Would this be my final moments of life, crying out in vain? A feeble mess lying in a pool of thick red liquid?

The last rush of adrenaline in my body pushed me to finish. I no longer had feeling or could move anything beneath the elbow. It seemed a near impossible task. I realized the only way was to use the hatchet I had been collecting ice shavings with to cleave through the bone. I felt nearly dead, and too weak to continue, as visions of life after this misdeed began to flood in with a rush of raw emotions.

Shock was setting in as I began to heave forth bile. I knelt on the floor, weak, frozen in place for a lapse of time, and stared into eternity. I found my conscious mind returning from the primitive state, as I was anemically dragging my weak body through the cabin to the next room. I reached for the small hatchet, with a far from steady hand. With a rush of brute force, I clinched below the tattered sinews and meat with right hand, and pulled down with a twisting motion, de-gloving more of the skin, and rupturing muscle. I found myself not even screaming any longer, completely depersonalized by the ordeal. It was almost as if I were watching myself perform some primeval surgery.

With the bloody bone exposed, I took several swings with what strength I could muster. The erosion within stood no chance against the tiny ax. I swear I could almost feel those bastards trying to migrate as I finished the deed. Hindsight tells me I should have just begun the task with the hatchet, but the madness controlled me like a puppet, and I danced at its will.

My dangling dead arm fell upon the floor in a lifeless lump, and the gravity of the situation rested its full weight upon me. I fell to the floor, darkness swirling around me as I faded into oblivion.

I came to, freezing, dizzy, and utterly confused; feeling as if death himself were standing over me. I heard dark whispers on putrid breath, that we were to meet soon. I tried to stand but fell upon one knee and stumbled clumsily into the washroom. A trail of my life's blood painted the floor behind me.

A dull ringing permeated my ears, as I gazed into the mirror. The paltry, dying light made fear and exhaustion known in every crack and crevasse of my complexion. My pupils resembled some sort of accursed looking glass, revealing a deep darkness. One that could rival the deepest miasmic pit of the underworld.

My dilated eyes widened, as terror wrapped its malicious hands around my throat.

I realized I had begun to feel an itch.

Deep within my left eye-socket.

DARK DISCOURSE

by N.W. Buchanan
artwork by Brett Gray

"I can't find it…the spark of motivation, of creativity that I need to write…" This was the thought I muttered aloud that fateful rainy eve not so long ago, the night that my entire world—nay, my very existence! —ceased to be, yet became so much more.

I was sitting hunched over my desk like so many nights before, pondering my next step. My deadline was creeping ever closer, and I had nothing. Not even an outline for my next story. I could hear the shouts of my editor already, berating me for yet another late article or hastily thrown together passage dripping with clichés and misnomers. I dredged through the vault that was my mind, searching for even the faintest thread of thought worth putting to paper.

I was close to abandoning hope when I felt the oddest sensation, as though a shard of ice had been placed upon my shoulder, moving slowly upward. Barely had this icy chill settled into the nape of my neck when I had a sudden fit of creativity.

The words leapt forth onto the page, spewing forth at an almost terrifying pace. I pounded feverishly away at the typewriter. Added to the rain rattling on the roof, the clacking of keystrokes created a deafening cacophony in my small bedroom. I had finished my entire article—and started what could've easily become a novel—before I stopped to read over the words.

There seemed to be something off about them, something wrong with the words themselves. The letters were somehow a darker black than I had ever thought possible.

Skimming the article, I took note of the rather dark leanings of what I had written. In its entirety, it seemed a far more, dare I say, sinister handiwork than I had ever proscribed to paper. I proceeded to examine it more thoroughly. It was indeed a startling read, though I had barely read half of it when my undertaking was interrupted by a most disturbing event.

"Quite the novella you've managed to jot down there, my good man," came the hoarse utterance from the dark.

"Who…who's there?" I stammered, nervously scanning the room. And with that, a creature stepped forth from the shadows enveloping the corner of my room nearest the door.

It was nearly seven feet tall, with quite a wide frame. It seemed to be covered in shiny black scales. Their edges glistened in the lamplight, all manner of red, green, gold and silver. The creature's skull narrowed nearly to a point at its chin and widened near the crown, where something akin to a ram's horns, of a rather dull ivory color, protruded from either side. As it stepped forth from its resting place, it stretched out one of its long arms—which ended in a rather claw-like hand, albeit with a mere three fingers. With this outstretched arm, it waved, bowing over in a semblance of dignified grace.

My mouth hung agape at the sight of such an imposing being—and that it had appeared from the shadows themselves.

"I was merely remarking on the fine literature you seem to have most recently produced there, M. _____," uttered the being as it rose from its bow.

"How do you know my name?"

The thing let out something akin to a chuckle, though it sounded more like the crunching of gravel than a lighthearted exultation.

"I am aware of far more than simply your name, my dear friend. But that is not important at this moment. It would seem as though, before my arrival, you were bereft of inspiration, struggling to release the flow of ideas from your mind. Seemingly, my presence was greatly needed if you were to have any hope of completing your fast-approaching deadline, no?"

My jaw slackened at this horrid thing, as it stared into my eyes and beyond. It flashed its glimmering teeth. Several rows of milky fangs appeared, as the creature proceeded with its discourse. It continued, explaining that its mere presence had offered a wellspring of inspiration to many writers in years past. The names that it revealed to me were those of the literary greats, the masters. (I believe it best if I keep these names to myself, for the revelation of even a few of these would cause no small scandal.)

Dumbfounded by the abundance of information my guest was unleashing upon me, I was jarred back to life by a long pause. I begged its pardon, as I seemed to have missed its last statement.

"Quite alright, monsieur. I was merely offering my continued services. In exchange for a small…trade. A slight token of your appreciation, if you would be ever so kind."

I was immediately set back on edge by this statement.

"But…I am in a rather difficult position," I mumbled. "What manner of token would be sufficient for such a grand boon as endless inspiration?"

Again, I was met with that gravelly sound, which I once more took to be laughter.

"Oh, no," it began. "Not endless, as all but a very few things in this great existence of ours are without end. But I can offer you no brief period of ephemeral creativity. I would simply ask that you forfeit unto me…" It paused, as if mulling over the right word. "Your soul," the being finally said, with what appeared to me a slight grin at the edges of its mouth.

I was more taken aback than I had been all evening at such a severe request. What exactly would it desire such a thing for? How would this transaction even begin to take place?

My gaze strayed for the first time from my sizable companion and hovered about the window. Rain continued to pour down in a deluge, soaking the city in a thunderous roar. We stayed there, both devoid of motion, for a long while.

"For how long?" I asked at last.

Another gravel chuckle was the response. I interrupted to clarify that I was speaking, of course, of my soon-to-be newly claimed inspiration.

"Ah, I see," replied the thing. "Three of your years. Three of your years, you shall enjoy endless inspiration and boundless creativity. All yours, in exchange for the paltry matter that is your soul. And really, of what use is it to you anyway?"

A faint grin emerged from this last question.

I further mulled the matter over. It was right, wasn't it? It wasn't as though I really seemed to be doing much with my "soul" anyway. And—think of it—if I was able to put down such words to paper in a matter of hours, imagine what I could accomplish in three years.

My mind made up, I stuck my hand out to shake the creature's three-fingered claw. There was no doubt in my mind now as to its grin. A huge smile tore across its face. It reached forward and clasped my sweaty palm. I felt another shiver, identical to the one that had preceded my inspired writing earlier in the evening.

Nearly instantaneous was the change I felt in myself. My mind seemed to burst with all manner of clever ideas. I was consumed by my immediate need to expel them forth onto paper.

The being gave another theatrical bow and thanked me for the transaction, promising to return in three years to retrieve his half of the bargain.

And now, here I was yet again: in my usual spot at my desk in the dim light of my bedroom. Furious were the keystrokes as I rushed to finish one last manuscript. I was all too aware of the date circled on my desk's calendar: three years to the very day of the trade that had granted me so much wealth. Thirty-one novels, one hundred and seventeen short stories, innumerable articles in various newspapers, magazines and the like. Finally, it would come to an end—snatched away from me, along with my everlasting soul.

Terror at this thought had begun to seep into the recesses of my mind. What would become of me? Would I continue on, unfazed by my lack of soul? Or would I be a mere husk, devoid of any emotion or meaning? I was gripped by these black thoughts as I heard an all too recognizable voice from behind.

"I hope I have found you in good health once more, M. _____?" said the demon as it stepped forth once more from the shadows of my room.

I merely nodded a solemn look upon my face.

"Well then, it seems as though the time has come. I would be much obliged if I could receive my fair compensation for the assistance I have provided you over these three years."

My mind raced. I was horrified at myself for having made such a bargain. Curse the death of inspiration that had condemned me to this fate!

But wait. Perhaps there was another way. Yes! What if I were to make a new bargain, find some way out of this unholy contract that I had felt forced into taking part?

"Perhaps not!" I cried. "Perhaps we can arrange another form of payment?"

My efforts were rebuked with a great sound like the crushing of gravel as the beast shook its head.

"Certainly not. We made a bargain, and I intend to claim my reward," replied the foul thing as it drew closer to me.

I felt yet more terror, if such an idea can even be imagined, as its hot breath swirled in my face. The demon loomed over me, drawing ever closer, with the obvious intent of cleaving my soul from its earthly abode. I flinched and stumbled backwards into my desk. The outstretched fingers of my left hand clasped something. Without a second thought, I swung it up at the beast as it drew nearer to me.

As it met with the demon's right eye, I realized it was the glass I had been sipping from. It shattered on impact and green liquid spewed forth, flooding over the wound. The demon let out an unearthly howl as it stumbled back, clutching at its face.

Seeing my opportunity, I seized the typewriter on my desk. I lunged forward and brought the machine down upon the creature's head with a horrid crunch.

The first strike brought the demon to its knees. The second slumped it onto all fours. I struck again and again with the fervor only a cornered, terrified man can muster. Finally, after I faced no more resistance, heard no more cries of anguish from the thing, I looked down upon it.

Its skull—and my beloved typewriter—were smashed to pieces in a pool of the most ebony blood I had ever laid eyes upon. Reaching down to ascertain whether I had indeed brought about the beast's startling demise, I laid my hand upon its shoulder and felt the most appalling and calamitous feeling that had ever washed over me.

I recoiled in fright from the carcass and tried to regain my faculties. Patting myself twice over to check for physical injury, I was pleased to find none, although I did feel a pain in my belly as an immense hunger came over me. I stepped over the corpse that now sprawled across my bedroom floor as though it were some morbid bearskin rug and proceeded to the door.

What harm could it bring for me to prepare a snack while I determined the best course of removal of this awful thing? I wondered to myself as I walked down the steps toward my kitchen.

Within a few moments, I found myself making quite an impressive sandwich. But devouring it did nothing to sate the hunger which rattled my body to its core. After a second hastily prepared sandwich, I felt even weaker than before. Fear crept back into me.

How was such a thing possible? Perhaps this was some odd defense mechanism of the demon's?

And then, as I looked down at my left hand, I found it was cut, presumably by the shattering of glass when I first struck the demon. Mixed with the drying red blood was a deep ebony-hued liquid.

Nearly collapsing, I bemoaned the hunger pains that coursed through my belly. How long before this insatiable hunger finally claimed my life?

Just when I had resigned myself to starvation, I smelled what could possibly be the most amazing scent I had ever breathed, an aroma that somehow instantaneously communicated a sense of hope. I felt if I could find the source of this scent and devour it, it would put an end to my hunger.

I hurled myself from my chair with a burst of energy only a man given a new lease on life can know. I bolted for the door. Scanning the street, I found that the night's darkness seemed a bit brighter than I remembered. It was less of a veil, more as though I were peering through a looking glass.

Then I saw, lying not far from my door, a body. It appeared that a vagrant had collapsed there, struck down by lack of sustenance, more likely than not. I was dumbstruck with horror at my second corpse of the evening before I realized that the otherworldly scent that had first drawn me out of my home seemed to be wafting from the man's lifeless body. I noticed something more: a small cloud of grayish blue floating over the poor soul's body.

"But…it's not!" I nearly shouted, stifling myself at the last moment so as not to draw undue attention to myself.

"He's not a poor soul," I whispered. "That is the soul."

I reached toward it, feeling it draw closer to my grasp. It glided silently into my hand.

I glanced warily around the street once more. Seeing not even the faintest trace of life, I looked back to the periwinkle cloud in my hand. With a sigh of conjoined relief and shame, I brought the cloud to my lips.

My mouth began to water as I prepared to feast on the dead man's soul. Licking my lips, I scampered back to my little apartment.

I have no doubt that you, gentle reader, can easily ascertain what has sustained my life on this mortal plane since then. With that I must draw my tale to an early close, as I have pressing business to attend to. You see, there is a young novelist who lives down the road from here, and rumor has it he is facing a bit of writer's block. And as I have learned these past few years, the most delectable meals are those acquired through a bargain.

BENUMBED

by Rachael Alexandra

I cry out in sorrow,
For love is my sorrow,
My sorrow, is my love.
I dance in the bitter sweetness.
I swim through the locks,
So jagged and cold.
Frozen cracks
Sharp buoyant daggers.
The gelid flow caresses me
Much like a heartless lover.
Fingers made of needles,
Hands made of blades.
Stroking me softly with
Such gentle brutality.
Coldly gaining entrance to my hollow,
With an invisible hand
You cannot push away.
Swimming in the frozen locks,
Trying to catch my breath.
It burns in my chest.
I start to sink and falter,
Submerging slowly.
This aqueous force
Over my mouth,
Forcing its way
Down my throat.
Like a cold cruel lover,
Taking what they need,
Then throwing you away.

TRILLIUM
by Rachael Alexandra

I am righteous screaming beauty, with my wicked scarlet ways.
The words that are spoken, you may never hear.
They are carried on the wind, in a language you may never know.
As my mouth fills with pollen, I choke on its sweetness.
Waiting for the toils of time to take their toll, so I may perish.
Only to come back in the spring, reborn and recharged.
Ready to hail the forest floor with my floral call, and cloak of carmine charms.
Once again.

"Kisses Kept" by Socar Myles

KISSES KEPT

by Rachael Alexandra

When I dream,
I dream of falling stars…

Stars falling
and
crossing…

Like the love you could never have,
And the kiss you could never steal…

R
 a
  i
   n
    i
     n
      g

D
 o
  w
   n

Like the tears from your eyes,
Like the pieces of your heart…

Pouring down such exquisite pain

INTERVIEW WITH
DOPPIO MUSIC

Hey Tim and Brittany! Thanks again for coming back to Outpost 28, Issue #2 for a follow-up interview. When we last spoke about Doppio in 2013, you guys were coming off the release of your self-titled album and the success of the track "The Battle." Since that time, how has the band grown?

Hey Dean, thank you for having us back; was a pleasure last time. From a growth perspective, I think we've come to be conscious of our sound more than we may have been in the past. It's an interesting thing hearing sounds in your head that turn into songs. It's all inevitably influenced in some way or another by your own personal taste, but you hope to put your own mark on it as well. We spent parts of 2014/2015 recording in Kentucky and had a great time there. Something about what I was writing left me unsatisfied though, and at some point, we began to hone in on what it was that made "The Battle" a unique sound. From there, the songs that comprise the EP we're currently recording at Sucker Punch Recording Co with Mark Williams quickly took shape.

To compliment the previous question, what have you two struggled with in terms of staying creative, yet keeping to your own style? Have there been any other obstacles that you have had to overcome?

In terms of keeping our own style, I try to limit what I listen to these days. To be honest, I don't listen to a whole lot of music through a given day. Things that I have been listening to are Chopin, Glenn Miller, Ray Charles, Django

Reinhardt, Etta James, Cole Porter to name a few. Mozart's Concerto 21 in C major is almost unbeatable. Those are sounds that I feel are so timeless, and to immerse myself in them draws a lot of feeling out, and certain ideas (the way they thought about things musically) have probably found their way into aspects of the songs on the EP we're recording.

Doppio's songs have been all over the place, including T.V. shows and big-name commercials. Can you talk about how all that amazing exposure was sparked and where you think it will lead?

We're extremely fortunate to have our songs in the hands of a publisher that we consider the best in the industry, Spirit Music Group. The people we work with there are some of the most genuine folks I've come across in my life, and they all possess great talents in having an ear for what will work with what regarding songs and the various forms of media that exist today. Where it will lead? Every once in a while, I wonder what it's all for...is it to reach as many ears as possible and have a chance to share a certain perspective, a certain shaded lens to peer through the looking glass at life? I used to feel this more a few years ago. Now I think it's just to keep on being in a position that allows me to keep writing songs. The writing is the best part.

Now that you guys have a child, have you found that he has influenced your style any? For example, when my kids were younger, their interests had a significant impact on my work and sent me into a very colorful, fairy-tale phase with my artwork and writing. Most of the time I just write and draw about dark and evil stuff! Have you experienced a similar phenomenon?

I was taking an Uber car home one night recently and struck up a conversation with the driver about this subject. What I learned is that our son, Jack, has inevitably made us realize our sound and drive toward that. Kurt Vonnegut said something along the lines of, "We are who we pretend to be, so we must be careful who we pretend to be". I think there's truth to that, but when I'm around my son, it's impossible to be anyone but 100% myself, and that's refreshing. There's no doubt it's rubbed off into the music.

How has the studio process been working for Doppio?

The studio is a creative playground. The goal for me has always been to get the sound out that I'm hearing in my head. Mark at Sucker Punch is brilliantly gifted in many ways and has a good knack for being open enough to operate on the same plane in the studio. It's a rewarding process, and one that's addictive.

What type of venues is Doppio playing in these days and do you prefer to play in smaller settings, or larger clubs?

It's been a pleasure to be the house musician/singer at the Ritz Carlton Pentagon City for the past year. Playing to a room of different people every night forces you to become quick on your feet while performing. I think the performer

who gets out there and does it night after night instead of just occasionally finds his/her stride at a much faster pace. Regarding the size of a room...doesn't seem to matter much as long as the energy of the room is one that's conducive to performing well.

Time for the question where you plug your forthcoming EP!

We're beyond eager to finish the songs on the EP up and get them out. We've been sharing studio footage each week from our Facebook and Instagram pages (if you haven't given one or the other a "like" yet, we'd be eternally grateful to ya if you did so ;)) We're getting close to the finish line and will be sharing a release date soon!

Congratulations to both of you with all your success and once again, I really appreciate the opportunity to ask you a few questions for this issue of Outpost 28. I am certain that 2018 with be an amazing year for Doppio!

Back at you and yours as well. We've always been fans of your work, and at times have drawn inspiration from it. Somehow our two worlds collided with this batch of songs, and when I look at your pieces now I'm taken to the world of the characters who took shape in our EP. Cheers to you, my friend.

INTERVIEW WITH
JASON WALTON

Jason, thanks again for returning to Outpost 28 for Issue #2. A lot has happened in your world since we last spoke in 2013. I still cry myself to sleep each night because of the fate of Agalloch, but that aside, you are still as productive and successful as ever. You guys formed KHôRADA from the break of Agalloch, but can you speak to the other personal projects you have going on?

Yes. Even though I am not on the road as much as I was when Agalloch was active, my musical career is as busy as ever. Of course, you already mentioned KHôRADA, but in addition to that I am busy with my mixing studio, Earth in Sound, as well as my eponymous experimental noise project, also Snares of Sixes, Sculptured and my newly launched podcast "I Hate Music." There are usually a few other projects going on as well, but those are my main focus at this time.

With all of your musical and creative projects, are you still diversifying with your litigation work, or are you completely devoted to your creative outlets now? In our 2013 interview I had left my day job to pursue just art and writing. Ironically, I am now back to a 40-hour a week, day job but doing much more writing and art than I ever did before. It's weird how it works out.

I still have a day job in Litigation Support, yes. Years ago, I cut back to part time work to focus more energy on my music, specifically Agalloch. I am still working only part time in Lit Support and the rest of my time is occupied with music, my podcast and family. Although I never quit my day job entirely, I feel that reducing my hours at my day job

was the right move, instead of quitting altogether. I find that having something other than art to focus on is very important. It keeps me grounded and saves me from being exhausted by my creative endeavors. I have known others who have quit work entirely and I fear greatly the effect on my music from external pressures, such as paying bills. I refuse to make artistic decisions based on financial reasons.

How have you grown as a musician from your experiences with your bands over the last few years? I find that most real growth, in any area in life, is learned from making mistakes. Can you reflect a little about a mistake you have made in recent years that you learned and grew from?

I learn the most just from doing. Touring as much as Agalloch did has been the best and most invaluable teacher, and of course making records and just simple longevity. Learning from experiences. Of course, as you say, mistakes are invaluable as well for growth. I can't think of one particular mistake I made that informed who I am as a musician now. I think it is more of a gradual and general process than something drastic that sticks out in your mind. On the other hand, in the music business, I've learned some hard lessons about trust and placing value on your work. If you don't value your work, no one else will, and most of the time, the labels, promoters, and managers need you more than you need them. In many cases the artist has the power, they just don't realize it.

What types of literally works inspire your musical ideas? What books are you reading right now just for the fun of it?

Literature and the written word have always been a huge influence on me. The works of Anthony Bourdain were a large influence on the Self Spiller record, Agalloch drew influence from many authors and I am constantly reading. Lately when I do not have my nose in a book about the Ramones, I am reading Karin Tidbeck, "Justine" by Marquis De Sade or works by Penny Rimbauld.

Once again, Jason, thanks so much for coming back and being a part of Outpost 28, Issue #2. I really appreciate your time and I hope 2018 is an awesome year for you personally, your family, your personal projects, and the new KHôRADA album.

Thank you, and thanks for asking me to be a part of this once again. Cheers!

INTERVIEW WITH
BEASTMAKER

Trevor, I really appreciate you taking the time out of your schedule to be a part of Outpost 28, Issue #2. I met you and John during last year's NecronomiCon in Providence, Rhode Island. You two stopped by for a few minutes to check out some of my artwork and I was struck by how laid back and approachable you guys are. I immediately pulled up some of your songs and was blown away by the old school metal style. I am sure you hear the Sabbath and Electric Wizard comparisons all the time, but I would like to look at it from a literary angle. Being that we met at a Lovecraft convention, has the work of H.P. Lovecraft influenced any of the lyrics or dark atmospheres in your songs?

All though I like Lovecraft none of my songs are influenced by his literary works. Most of my influences for Beastmaker come from old movies like Tombs of the Blind Dead, Black Sunday, Colors of the Dark, etc. Also, strangely I share a Birthday with Hitchcock so sometimes I throw in some dark mystery into my lyrics. Maybe it is time for me to write some Lovecraft inspired doom. I do own a few Lovecraft books, but it's been quite some time since I've read them, and his work would go hand in hand with what I do. Maybe Reanimator would be a good theme.

You mentioned to me that Beastmaker is your moniker and that its concept was your creation. The band is clearly doing really well, but I would like to ask you of an instance during the early days of its creation that was difficult. Are there any memorable examples of hurdles you guys had to overcome?

Everything is a hurdle. The music business is a hurdle. I think the biggest challenge Andy and I faced in the earlier days was finding a bass player. The other huge hurdle was getting a demo album put together that we could be proud of. Now days it's breaking down and missing flights. You just don't ever know what problems you are gonna have to endure.

How did you, John and Andre form Beastmaker? Did you guys work together in other bands previously, or did you form Beastmaker first and then seek them out?

Andre and I have been friends for 15 years now and we played in many different bands together over the years from Math Rock, to Dirty Rock n Roll, Thrash metal. Very broad spectrum of bands. John was in a band called Blind Bison and their drummer bailed and we thought well John is a great guitarist maybe he will play bass. He accepted and that was a little over three years ago. We've now done multiple USA tours and two full Europe tours. Played festivals and have two full length albums under our belts.

Since the 2015 release of your first EP, You Must Sin, can you talk about how Beastmaker has grown either lyrically or in musical style? How would you compare that release to your most recent full-lengths?

I don't think it's our intention to really grow. I think as you move on musically you just get better at what you do. Things get tighter and stronger. We just aren't that project that is going to be doing a lot of different stuff. We are gonna keep it slow and heavy. Lyrically I tell stories in Beastmaker. It's all short little horror movie ideas or paying homage to great horror films that inspire me to write the songs. I can definitely say from our first full length "lusus naturae" to our latest full length "inside the skull" there are subtle differences some of the songs have a different beat but mostly we stick to old school doom metal. We have fun with that and that's what matters the most to us.

Haunt is another creation of yours. What can you tell us about that project?

Haunt is a much more melodic upbeat **NWOBHM** influenced project. I just released an **EP** on Shadow Kingdom Records called "Luminous Eyes" and we are currently following up with a full length as we speak. It's definitely a throwback style of metal. If you like bands like Angel Witch, Diamond Head, Ozzy Osbourne (80's), Def Leppard, Early Hagar. This is something along those lines. Lyrically I speak more about my own personal life in Haunt or stuff that has happened to people I know. Definitely more songs about Love. I wanted to do something the opposite of Horror, so Haunt was my answer.

AUTHOR AND ARTIST BIOS

AYESHA AHMAD

Ayesha Ahmad is a part time author, full time development practitioner (fancy words for working in the typical cubicle workplace), and a full-time mommy. She lives in Islamabad, Pakistan with her family. Ayesha writes short stories and is currently working on her first novel. She is passionate about animals and the environment and is an avid reader of all types of fiction, and in particular science fiction and fantasy.

RACHAEL ALEXANDRA

I live in the frigid northeast, where winters are cold, and the summer is fleeting. I write some poetry and some prose, I also read a fair bit as well. I take pictures of things, many times of small things or things that I've grown, but I dabble in just about everything. I enjoy gardening and landscaping. I love my pets and my family. I currently work as a florist. I am simply a small-town girl, with a rich emotional life and a creative streak.

www.myeyedelight.com

JAKE BAUER

Jake is an avid reader and writer; eater and chef. He, while no longer a student at VCU, still lives in his hometown of Richmond in a quiet alley with his lovely girlfriend and partner, surrounded by their books and plants that seem smarter than they should be. This is his second time appearing in Outpost 28, and he looks forward to more opportunities for creative outlets in the future!

DAVID BONNEYWELL

Dave is a British born make up effects artist. He started in the industry in 1992 at Image Animation and was workshop supervisor there until 2002. He has since worked with many companies around the world including Neil Courbould, Creature Effects, Spectral Motion, Tony Gardner, Gorton Studio, Millennium FX and BGFX as well as being a freelance designer, writer and production artist. He does all aspects of prosthetics from make-up application to mould making, is a highly skilled sculptor and creature/character designer and supervised the effects on many of his credits. Dave has worked on many high-profile feature films like Event Horizon, Ronin, Dog Soldiers, Beyond Borders, Troy, Oliver Stone's Alexander, Seed of Chucky, 28 Weeks Later, Harry Potter and the Half-Blood Prince, Hellboy 2: The Golden Army, and Clash of the Titans. His many television credits include Dr. Who, Wizards Vs. Aliens, and Game of Thrones. He now lives in Portugal and although still very active in the film and TV industry, is concentrating more on his own art and teaching through EffectArt, a company he founded with his wife Rita. **www.effectart.com.pt**

MICHAEL BRACK

I am a self-taught painter and illustrator currently living in Paris. I debuted by doing fantasy and fantastic/horror illustrations for magazines, and also did a few book covers. I am now focusing on painting, trying to create intriguing, strange or unsettling images, with a particular interest in composition and lighting. **www.michaelbrack.com**

N.W. BUCHANAN

Nathanael W Buchanan is an avid horror fan, heavily influenced by Edgar Allen Poe and H.P. Lovecraft. Born and raised in Newport News, VA, he has been driven by the occult from childhood after watching films such as Halloween and Friday the 13th. After beginning to write in early 2011, Buchanan's tales of darkness and despair have begun to creep into the light, and our minds.

CHRISTA CARMEN

Christa Carmen's work has been featured in a myriad of anthologies, ezines, and podcasts, including *Unnerving Magazine, Fireside Fiction, Year's Best Hardcore Horror Volume 2, Tales to Terrify,* Third Flatiron's *Strange Beasties,* and Alban Lake's *Only the Lonely.* Her debut collection, "Something Borrowed, Something Blood-Soaked," will be available in August 2018 from *Unnerving.* **www.christacarmen.com**

DOPPIO MUSIC

Doppio Music is a duo that plays intergalactic baroque pop. **www.doppiomusic.com**

ANDY FAIRHURST

Andy currently lives in gorgeous North Wales with his wife and 3 kids, but he grew up in Wolverhampton. He specializes in alternative movie posters and pop culture art prints. He has done many works for Disney, Lucasfilm, Marvel, 20th Century Fox and the BBC, amongst others, and worked with galleries such as Bottleneck Gallery and Grey Matter Art and Iam8bit Gallery in the USA. **www.andyfairhurstart.com**

BRETT GRAY

A traditional artist, Brett Gray has been drawing since he was old enough to pick up a pencil and studied Fine Art at the University of Kentucky and Western Kentucky University. Using charcoal on paper to create his nightmarish portraits and macabre scenes, his inspirations range from icons of art, literature, and film, like H.R. Giger, H.P. Lovecraft, and Guillermo del Toro, to folklore, horror literature and movies, and the murky depths of his own subconscious. Brett began selling his artwork in September of 2010 and has since sold several of his originals to private collectors and completed multiple commissioned works. His first sale, a Lovecraftian piece entitled Night of the Old Ones, is now in the private collection of Jenette Kahn, former president of DC Comics. He currently resides in Kentucky with his wife Sheryl and their three cats. **website: www.brettgrayart.com www.facebook.com/BrettGrayArt**

VICTOR JOHNSTON

Rugged handsomeness, a sultry voice, and bountiful charisma could have dotted Victor Johnston's life with fame and fortune. However, with a quest to have a deep mastery of the written word, he now sets out on the next great journey in life. An avid fan of both oral storytelling and scribed work, this jack-of-all-trades once hosted a weekly paranormal podcast, which focused on the telling of the darker tales from man's existence. The garnered expertise of keeping listeners on the edge of their seats is funneled into all of his works; be it written, spoken, or musical. The publication of *Hand of Fate* is Victor Johnston's first venture into the echelons of printed work, and seemingly the Rosetta stone for much to come.

DEAN KUHTA

Dean lives in Richmond, VA, and likes to draw and write stuff. He is the creator, curator, and supreme overlord of Outpost 28. **www.deankuhta.com**

SOCAR MYLES

Socar Myles lives in Vancouver, and enjoys drawing, looking at funny shapes made by worms on the pavement, and watching the local birds. **www. gorblimey.com**